Shattering the Glass Ceiling

Janet Kuypers

cyberWit.net

This book is for all who have lived through trauma,
and for all who have fought the uphill battle
for fairness and equality

I would like to thank all of the people who have shared their stories with me over the years, as often sharing is the first step toward both recovery as well as understanding and growth.

I would also like to thank the people who translated some of my poetry into other languages, including Jean Hellemans, Farid Mohammadi, and John Yotko. Thank you for helping me to share this poetry with people around the world.

Contents

No One Reports for Women

I would start this like a news reporter, saying
"Dateline, *your town here*",
but news about women's issues is nonexistent,
which makes women wonder
if concerns for women are nonexistent too.

Recently I heard reports from multiple women
who had been on birth control
for 99% of their fertile lives—
they contracted the most recent variant of Covid-19
    (and yes, they got vaccines and booster shots,
    making Covid-19 like getting a minor cold)
but these women noticed a week after recovery
    (two weeks before their period should arrive)
they started spotting, which didn't stop—
so after ten says, they asked around
                and found
that other women were having this trouble
with their reproductive health too,
and no one had researched how to solve it.

But really, think about it: who would have the time
to research something when they worked like mad
just to come up with a vaccine on such short notice?
No one has questioned men's fertility after Covid-19
and enough immunization to protect you from this...

But maybe the question should be this:
after women can now control their reproductive rights,
does that mean that after following their government's edicts
to "protect" themselves and inject themselves,
they'll still get sick, but, added bonus,
they'll bleed *daily* for it?
Because this is exactly the type of problem
women *don't* want to talk about in public
and trust me, this *shouldn't* be a problem
any woman should *ever* have to deal with.

When women sit alone in their corners
with no support for their *very* personal problems,
they don't know that other women go through this too.
That little level of sympathy
may assuage their feelings,
but it may amount to only a fleeting gesture
to know they're not alone—
for the more you realize how common this may be,
the more any rational woman would wonder
why something isn't being done
to solve what is becoming a real
bloody
problem.

When many women's solution is to search the Internet
they may start to panic when they read reports
that birth control may increase blood clots,
and Covid-19 may exacerbate that risk further,
but, surprise surprise, more research needs to be done
to solve anything for women,
and this *still* doesn't solve
this daily bleeding that men are stating is harmless
     (fine, but men aren't the ones bleeding every day).
So, this is beginning to sound more like
more of the same, women think,
we are in pain, and nothing is being done.

There may be theories that estrogen and progesterone
may play a role in the novel coronavirus
     (may this explain the Covid-19 reaction differences
     between feminine me and my masculine husband?)
but *taking* estrogen daily, could that effect
the vaccine, *or* the virus?
Well, it doesn't matter if one doctor after another
hears a stack of anecdotal evidence from their patients,
because stories aren't proof,
and women are all still stuck,
bleeding,
with no way to solve their medical problems.

And for the men out there
that don't want to think about women bleeding
(even though men have no problem
with the same women bearing and raising *their* children,
which women have to bleed monthly for to make happen),
similar stories arise with young women,
possibly wanting to have children one day,
missing their period *for four months*
after getting Covid-19, with irregular periods resuming
    (though when one woman talked to her doctor about it,
    they assumed it was from Covid-19, but to quote
    the patient, "none seemed too concerned about it.")

So, welcome to another case
of an unexpected medical problem
women are having that no one can explain...

I jokingly said
that I'd like to start this story
by saying "Dateline *(your town here)"*—
but maybe I should have said all along:
Dateline, *your neighborhood,* or
Dateline, *your street,* or
Dateline, *your home.*
Because after only now hearing
the now upswelling cries
of women who follow the rules
and do what's best for them—
women only suffer for it with no explanation, and
    (of course)
can't share their problems
in an effort to solve them.
If women *could* tell their stories
it may only be a stepping stone.
But if women *did* tell their stories,
you may only then realize
how serious
the problems women go though
can really be.

Like Nothing Ever Happened

In Waco, Texas
a grand jury
found enough
evidence
in the case
against a man
indicted on four counts
of sexual assault
to send the case
to trial.

Now, usually,
when a grand jury
sends a case
to trial,
that usually means
there's enough
evidence
to convict.

But I just heard
on the news
that instead,
he pled
no contest
to one charge
of unlawful restraint
in return
for the dismissal
of four charges
of sexual assault.

With this plea
from this fraternity
president rapist,
who had nothing
to offer the state
in a plea deal,
he gets this lower charge
in exchange
for
counseling,
a $400 fine
     (which is less
     than the fine
     for leaving
     a disabled car
     to get help),
plus three years
probation.
Added bonus,
if he stays clean
until probation's over,
his record
would be
expunged.

This means
he wouldn't have to
register as a sex offender —

it would be
like nothing ever happened.

This woman
was repeatedly
raped,
strangled,
and left
for dead
face down
in the dirt.
She was brought
to the hospital,
where they
called the police.
There's an enormous
amount of evidence.
A conviction
is almost sure.

Four counts of
sexual assault.
And they treat it
like nothing ever happened.

Women think
we've shattered
the glass ceiling,
but we still
have to shatter
the mentality
that woman are objects
and rape is not a crime.
We try to plead our case,
but nothing ever happens.

Maybe we women
have to shatter
more than ceilings,
but also men's mentality.
Maybe we should
even shatter
a few of your bones,
the way you shatter our souls
with every act of rape.

Shattering your bones
would not even
cross the line
you rapists cross
with your misogyny
and violence.
Is that what we're left with?
Is that what we have to do?
Should we start to get down
as low as you
to start
to try
to even
the score?

If we're so equal,
is it not our turn
to exact our revenge?

(Former Baylor University Phi Delta Theta president and student Jacob Walter
Anderson was arrested and charged with sexual assault in 2016.)

Escaping Rapeugees

I was hoping
the world for women
was turning the corner,

that the world
may finally have evolved
to respect us women.

How silly of me.

Remember girls,
hold your own
out alone at night,

and don't assume
if men give you drinks
it's just because

they're nice.
Some men are good,
I know it's true,

but that doesn't mean
the battle is over
and you can feel safe.

Watch your back,
walk fast, check
over your shoulder.

You still work
harder for less
pay than men,

and the men
probably still
expect you to cook

and clean for them,

birth and raise
their babies too.

Because that's your job,
to do everything — and
don't forget to smile.

I mean, if you think
you're in the clear
and have nothing to fear,

you can be raped
by people you trust
as well as strangers...

Because keep in mind
that Europeans
now have a name

for the Syrian
and Muslim refugees
they've taken in:

rapeugees. Because
Muslim migrant
mass sexual assaults

seem to be
the raping theme
in twenty sixteen.

So, women...
You think you're safe?
Think again.

Because now we've learned
that we can be raped
for being nice.

So, keep a vigilant eye,
and keep up the good
work, ladies.

A Woman Talking About Her Rapist Friend

He was my friend, and we had been
through a lot together, our psychological
ups and downs,

but he mixed drinks exceptionally well
at his college frat parties, and his
ice-blue eyes

always spoke the truth to me. It's amazing
to think that the only reason we ever met
was because one day

he wore a turtleneck that prefectly
matched his eyes, and I had to tell him.
I don't know why

he put up with my mood swings, with my
self-destructive social life and man-hating,
normally he didn't

care about women, never gave their opinions
much thought, just tried to get them
drunk at parties,

maybe he knew that and that's why he
listened to me. Then for a few years
our friendship

drifted, we didn't see each other much,
I heard through the grapevine that he was
failing in school.

Then one day, out of the blue, he comes
over and he has two black eyes. And he
says to me

that when he was in the parking garage
two guys came and beat him up, and one
of them said,

you raped my girlfriend. And then he looked
at me and said, and you know, looking back,
he was right.

I raped her. And I know he wanted sympathy, he wanted to hear me say something,
but I couldn't.

And he said, I know this has to be hard for
you to hear, but I wanted to tell you. I know
it was wrong.

A part of me wanted to hate him. A part of
me thought that if he was my friend I would
be condoning

what he did. And a part of me thought that
our friendship made him realize what he
had actually done.

I tried to be there for him. I wasn't much
good at it. Eventually, he moved away.
I didn't try

to lose touch with him. But it's just that a
part of me is still trying to figure out if I
can be his friend.

Sometimes you just lose touch with someone, sometimes that's all you can do.

Coslow's

I am back
at my old college
hang-out

years later

sharing some beers
with an old friend

then i remember
being there
with a friend
who used to
work there

she told me about the
women's bathroom

in all my years
I had never
been there

she said
women write on the wall
at the left
of the stall
women write
that they've been raped

they name names

there were arrows
pointing
to other women's
messages
saying
"i've heard this before"

first names
last names

when she told me
of this
years ago
i walked in
read the names
and wrote down one
of my own

i forgot about that wall
until now
and i am back
just yards away
from the
bathroom door

i get up
walk
open the door
years later

all the names are still there
jake jay josh larry matt scott

i can even still see
my own writing
it didn't take long
to find it

Raped with Words

I knew a woman
who went on a date
with a friend of mine,
and after the date
he talked about how great she was,
he told me how they talked about their future
and what they both wanted
he described the inside of her place,
but after he left messages for her repeatedly,
she never called him back again

saw this woman weeks later
at a Starbuck's
and she said she felt bad she had been avoiding hm
but she never wanted to see him again
because during their date
they never talked about what they wanted
he just talked about what he wanted
like how she wouldn't hold a job
she'd be taking care of the house
the man's the one that makes the money
and he even told her how many
of his children she would bear

she wouldn't let him into her home
(does that mean he was looking through her window?)
and she said that after the date
she showered for hours
because she felt like she had been raped

and you know, hearing her story
it made me realize
that you can rape someone
with words

Gasoline

The stench of gasoline makes me ill
as the song pounces through my brain
"I want you to want me
the way that I want you"
and I'm tired of fighting
I don't think I can fight anymore
but I have to
I can't let you do this
these are my rights
and you can't hurt me like this
"Then maybe I'll just force you"
you say
I push you away
I try to stop you
and all I keep hearing
is that damn song
I can't escape it
"I know that you need me
just tell me you want me
I want you"
I'm too angry to cry
and too frightened to scream
I shove, I move
but nothing stops you
"You are my sensation
a perfect temptation"
I wish that song would stop
I wish everything would stop
your touch scares me
and your stare haunts me
so I scratch and scream
until the novelty is lost for you
no
I will not tell you I want you
for I can't let you do this
these are my rights
and you just can't do this to me

the Room of the Rape

For almost two years when I walked up the nine stairs,
held on to the wooden railing whose finish was worn,
I'd pass the first door on the right.
My bedroom door was closed for one year, ten months and seven days.
I slept in the den across the hall.

One morning I woke, walked into the hall
and looked at the door. I turned around,
knowing I couldn't take it anymore,
walked into the den, folded the bed back into the couch,
and then walked into the hall, squarely facing
the door of the room.
A room in my house, that I let him go in to.
But when I woke up that morning, I told myself
that I wouldn't let him stop me today.

I turned the handle of the door. I heard a snap.
I slowly pushed the door open,
slowing it down to hear the hinges creak.
The shade to the small window in the corner was drawn,
so I stepped onto the parquet floor and turned on the light.

I felt the walls jump back in fear,
    fear of having to see the light again,
    then rush in on me in anger.
I saw the bed sheets rustle, get kicked
    and tossed to the ground again.
I tasted the sweat and I wanted to spit,
    but I couldn't. Something told me
    that wasn't what I was supposed to do.
My bedroom.
I saw the fists reach out from the walls
    and thought of the poster I drew
    of rebellion and rage
    that is tucked in the back of my closet.

I felt the muscles tense behind my eyebrows
I pursed my lips
I swallowed the sweat
My bedroom.
I felt the fists punching my stomach,
    grabbing my face, my arms, my hair,
    pulling my legs apart.
I felt my head against the pillows again
    as I tried to just push my face
    into the salt and the sheets
I heard the screams I never made
    echo inside me
    the screams that haunted me
I closed my eyes from the pain and the light
My bedroom.
I thought of the fist, the symbol for the
    communist work ethic
    to do what you're told,
    to disappear into society.

I opened my eyes.
The room was mine --
the sheets on the floor, the stains on the bed, the smell of Hell
and the photographs on the dresser.
I looked at the pictures
and found one of him, with his arms around me.
I picked up the frame,
ran my hand along the gilded edges.
Flakes of paint fell to the floor.
I opened the drawer of the dresser
and gently set it face down.
I turned around,
shutting off the light on my way out.
My bedroom.

Rape Education one

I sat in on a seminar
being held at a university
about acquaintance rape

when the woman behind the podium
asked if there were any other questions,
a woman raised her hand

she was a pretty woman

she asked what a woman
could do through the university
to prosecute the man

she sounded tough
she sounded professional

and the woman behind the podium
asked if this woman was raped

and she said yes

and the woman behind the podium
empathized with her,
told her she was raped
when she was thirteen

told her that she could tell this
certain department at the university
and they would bring a hearing on him

and then the woman behind the podium
asked, well, if you don't mind my asking,
when did this happen to you

and by the tone of the woman's voice
she was so calm so collected
I expected her to say
a few years ago

and her response was
six days ago

now, I know the healing process for rape
I've studied it in books
first there's denial, then anger, fear
some of these steps last for years

and here was this woman
so calm so collected
to tough so professional
and I just knew
that one day

all of her defenses would fall
and it would all hit her
and she would fall
apart

I felt like her mother

she was my baby
and I wanted to deliver her
from the pain
but there was nothing I could do
I felt so helpless

nothing I could have taught her
would prepare her for this

Rape Education two

I told a friend
that I worked for
acquaintance rape action groups

she confided in me
told me that she was raped
when she was sixteen

you see, it went like this:
her boyfriend was 23
she was just in high school
and she was drunk
and she didn't know what to do

and all I could think
was that more and more people
are telling me
stories like this

Rape Education three

I told a friend
that I worked for
acquaintance rape action groups

she told me she tried
to start a group of her own
at her college

her catholic college

and they told her she wasn't allowed
to do it
because acquaintance rape
is not a problem
here

she tried to write an article
about it for her paper
they wouldn't print it

what else was she supposed to do

Best Friend

"I had a best friend once,"
I said matter-of-factly,
as I stared into the palm of my hand.
You laughed my remarks off a sarcasm.
So I waited for a silence
so that I would have the thrill
of breaking it.
"I had a best friend once—
and he raped me."
There. You wanted to hear it.
How can you break the silence
now? I've taken away your weapons.
Have I taken away your compassion, too?
Tell me what good this knowledge
does you now.
Reminding me doesn't help,
and there's nothing you can do
to make the pain go away.
As you sit there in silence,
I wonder if there must be someone
who can say what needs to be said to me.
A best friend, maybe.
But if only a best friend
can help me now
then I would prefer
not to be helped.
I don't ever want to find
a best friend again.

Pushed Aside

No,
I don't feel
as if something was taken away from me.
He pushed himself through me
and he pushed everything that was inside of me
off to the side.
He just pushed me to the side,
and all I feel is a hole.
There is a void where he used to be:
it's always there,
and I wish that
like a hole in the wall
I could fill myself up with something
patch myself up with something
so that I would no longer have to feel.
But I can't.
Anything to repair my injuries
would only remind me that I was injured.
I only wish that
I could push myself back to where I used to be
where I should be
and fill the emptiness inside.
As I rest my hand on me
I want to push myself back to where I should be.
where I should be.
But I can't.
And every time I move,
every time I turn, or sit,
or cross my legs,
I feel the void.
And although the burning is less intense,
it is always there.
Where I was pushed aside—

A Socially Accepted Target

rape is connected
to the frustration produced
by living in this society

rape is anger
misdirected towards
a socially accepted target:
women

> Men and Politics Group,
> East Bay Men's Center,
> Statement on Rape

i didn't get the promotion i deserved
i work in a cubicle
the boss doesn't know my name
i put in too much overtime
this tie makes it hard to breathe

this traffic is always in my way
there's all these bills i have to pay

i'm angry all the time

and the damn kids are banging
their toys when i come home
and dinner is never on time
and your looks have just gone to hell
and i hate you

i just want a fucking beer, you bitch

it's all your fault

Killing, Loving, and the Power of Women

You can't help but love the look
of the Praying Mantis; the unique way it moves
is utterly fascinating to the eye.

But I had no idea that one of the
reasons I could fall in love with a Praying Mantis
was precisely because the woman

kills her mate during, or just after
they've finished their mating business. Because
really, what do you need him

around for anyway, after you got
yours? And the beauty of this kind of conquest
is that it happens across species,

and it happens from insects to
animals too. Some Black Widow Spiders are known
to kill their post-coital mates.

Female spiders even have larger
venom sacks. And the things is, female bees and wasps
have the stingers — not the males.

Yeah, you heard me right, those
male worker drone bees don't even have stingers.
And one female bee is chosen

when young to be queen, then is
raised by male bees until she rules over them all.
Female honey bees call the shots

in their caste system matriarchy,
in a female-centered hive, where the males only serve
for sexual reproduction. Also,

male insects and animals are
brightly colored to stand out to be better looking —
you know, to attract the females...

while the females stay at home
and take care of what's theirs. Even female octopi
strangle their male mates

when the deed is done. And the
female lion does the majority of hunting for its pride,
sometimes not even sharing their food.

Female Bonobos (chimpanzees)
are at the top of their group's social pyramid, the top
in their matriarchal society.

And get this one: in many societies
of the anglerfish, the male, which is smaller, literally
attaches himself to a woman,

and get this, starts to atrophy
until she is ready to use him for her reproductive needs.
If a male anglerfish doesn't

find a female, he will literally die.

So I don't know how it got so
messed up with us humans, we women have always been
the ones with the power, and now

we fight an uphill battle
because we've been thought of as less than human.
Tell that to Nefertiti or Pharaoh

Cleopatra is all I can think,
because somewhere along the line, men decided
to take over the world

while we only gave them a home,
gave them family and offspring to raise and flourish —
in the male's name, no less —

and what's our thanks?
For stopping killing you men, you've taken our humanity,
and for millennia we fight

for any rights back.
And sorry, but I don't know who made this deal,
but I didn't agree to it,

and I want my money back.

Quenching Anybody's Thirst

How do you respond
when someone calls you
a tall drink of water?
I mean,
when it comes
to the mentality
of old men like this,
I really
have no intention
of quenching
anybody's thirst.

from In the Air

Have you ever noticed that the air isn't normal air in an airplane?
I mean, there's just something about the air in the cabin that's different.
It's got a smell to it, that's the only way I can describe it.
A smell of all these people, maybe not going places, but getting away,
as fast as they can.

Once, when I was on a flight back from D. C., a flight attendant
walked by, stack of magazines in her hand, Time, Newsweek,
Businessweek, and I stopped her, asking what magazines she had.
And she replied, "Oh, these magazines are for men."
This is a true story.
And I asked her again, what magazines do you have.
I had already read Time, so I took Newsweek.

Objectifiable 2021

I've experienced it
for I don't know how many years,
men degrading women.

When I was walking
down the street today,
a man in an ugly mini-van
stuck his head out of his window
to holler for me

Wow, lucky me.
I'm still objectifiable.

But don't worry, objectification
Transcends physical proximity,
even in post-coronavirus times,
while many places are still closed...

I was interviewed on a Chicago radio station
where men could still post on a YouTube video
that

"I would like to see you
wear something
a bit more revealing.

You have a nice rack."

Because yes,
lucky us,
being as objectifiable
as we all are —
female objectification
even transcends
the Internet.

Yes, lucky me indeed.

Q L G six four seven

Was only a fourth of the way
on my four-mile walk,
my second walk of the day.

It was sixty degrees,
so I wore a tank top and long shorts
and I welcomed any breeze.

But just as I walked past
the high school at noon, a huge pick up truck
roared by, giving me a horn blast.

Okay, I know that sexism still lingers
but I thought, enough was enough
and I gave them the finger.

And I thought it was over,
but after I walked another ten feet
I saw the truck pull over.

I stopped walking
when they opened their door.
The driver got out,
closed his door,
leaned on his truck
and asked,

"Missy,
what was that for?"

And I thought, you're kidding me,
he was the one first in the wrong,
and he leaned on his pick-up truck
just waiting for me
to walk towards him...

So as I continued my pace

I said,
"I was reacting
to a stranger
objectifying a woman
in front of a high school,
you pervert."

Then I stopped walking.

He finally asked,
"Are you from the high school?"
And I replied,
"It's not a smart idea
to be honking your horn
at a woman walking by
as you pass a high school
in the middle of the day."

I started walking again,
slowly,
and as I got closer
he said,
"You not a part of the school.
Your tit's 're too big
to be a student there."

Which made me almost trip
in my stride.
But at only
ten feet away
I replied,
"Keep talking.
With every word
you're making yourself
sound even worse."

So I began to regain my pace
and he said,
"Why are you being so uptight?"
So I stopped,
three feet in front of him.

I turned my head only slightly,
and I read aloud.

"Q L G six four seven."

"What?" he asked.

"Just wanted to remember
the license plate number
of the misogynist
who stopped me today."

"The what?" he asked,
and before he could say anything else
I cut in.
"There's no word in the English language
for women who hate men,
but you men have mastered degrading us
and expect us to do nothing in return."

He didn't have an answer
for me explaining big words to him.

"I think you should go,"
I finally said,
and was pleased
that he didn't have any more worlds for me,
and I walked away.
I only had three miles to go
before it was all over... temporarily,
again.

Scratch the Surface

you don't have to pull out the Book for Men
to know how men degrade "the weaker sex"
or even assault women with the English language

hey, they can even try to make it sound nice
think it's a compliment to call us a honey
a fox, a pumpkin, their cougar, or even a hot chick

but if calling us food or animals is too degrading
I can be your babe, and I'm still your girl
I mean, calling us less than an adult can still degrade us

but I get furious when I'm wearing a tank top
you know, because it's hot outside
and a semi or a truck honks their horn

I mean, do they think honking their horn is a compliment?
or are they busy blowing their horn
to try to show off their big rig?

 I thought the Book for Men covered all the bases,
even with sex in terms men understand:
banging, hammering, nailing, screwing, scoring

but I was in a car, and because it was warm
I was wearing a tank top (again,
the truck driver's sexual turn on)

so I got honked at by a semi driver
while sitting in a car, going down the highway
and that's when I heard of one more term for women

someone informed me that after their truck horn blares
the truck driver will radio ahead to other semis
and tell them the color, make and model

of a car with a good-looking
seat cover

wow, a seat cover. thanks.
now we're reduced to good-looking upholstery
something you keep around to sit on

but we can't stay pretty
after you've kept us down for years,
before you get something prettier to replace us

so as I sit in this car
covering myself up whenever we're near a truck
I think about the Book for Men

with jokes objectifying women
or reminding us of a bush, a slit, a crack,
a box, a hole, or a farm implement, like

a hoe

but I'm telling you, baby doll
as thorough as that handbook seems
it doesn't even scratch the surface

Confident Women

I met up with an old friend of mine
for drinks last week. I knew her
in high school, although we weren't
close friends then. In those days she
needed therapy, had problems with drugs,
I think, or else it was just family
problems. I was a bit insecure myself,
shy, meek, scared of life. Since those days
we matured, we're now more independent,
self-confident, self-assured women.
It was good to see her again. She
just came back from camping in
Australia; although physically I had
gone nowhere, we both had our stories
to tell over a bottle or two of wine.
And we gossiped, she told me of the
handsome Australian man she fell for,
I told her of the roller-coaster I call
my romantic life. And we laughed.
And then the gossip changed, her
voice lowered, and sounding stern
but quiet, she told me of how a man
broke into her apartment one night
last summer and he tried to rape her,
and after kicking and screaming
in her underwear she managed to
break free and her attacker escaped.
She told me they found the man,
and the trial is scheduled for later
in the month. And she sat there, with
her wine glass in her hand, looking

so confident, as if she knew she
won this battle. Trying not to sound
corny, I told her I could give her
a hug. And she leaned on my shoulder,
and she cried, hiccupping as she
tried to catch her breath. They
would make her recount everything
on the stand, she said, and the defense
lawyers would try to make her sound
promiscuous because she slept
alone in her underwear. I told her I
would go with her to the trial. I told her
she is winning by speaking out.
Self-assured women. Confident women.
How confident are we supposed to be?

Keeps Repeating

I question   my turning the other cheek
when your violent strikes   just get stronger
and this painful history   keeps repeating itself

Meitnerium: For All We Women Must Do

written for the 1982 date Meitnerium was Synthesized for the First time

One woman fought a system
that didn't allow her schooling,
and worked as a scientist

She co-discovered nuclear fission,
Nazi Germany then went for her;
she escaped with her life

She taught us to always search
& discover, for this learning & growing
is what all we women must do

Opened the Door for All
Written 11/7, the 1867 birthday of Marie Curie

born in Warsaw,
the youngest of five,
she did well in school —
but it didn't matter
when women were not
allowed higher education

undeterred, she even
made deals with professors
to work there for free
so she could also
illegally go to school
before schooling in Paris

while there she found her love
in Pierre, they married,
gave each other bicycles
as wedding presents,
while she wore a black
dress to her wedding

so dirt wouldn't show
when she went back to work —
and work she did, separately
from Pierre, until she
discovered radioactivity,
and Pierre put his pride aside

and worked to help his wife...
after his accidental death,
it was a heartbreaking loss
for her, but she took over
his teaching post, making her
Sorbonne's first female professor

she discovered radioactivity
but also a new element, named
for her home country — and
in WWI she developed portable
x-ray devices they nick named
"Little Curies"

The Great War didn't get her,
but her love of her studies did,
as working with radiation so long
and keeping vials of Radium
in her lab pockets daily would be
too much, even for her genius

people truly admire Albert
Einstein, whom she worked with,
but... for women, and for all of
humankind, this woman faced
more obstacles than most —
and opened the door for all

Extension of "Him"

Written 11/21, on the 1929 birthday
of feminist writer Marilyn French

When I got married,
I thought about
my having to take
my husband's last name
and use it as my own,
destroying my own history
and now calling myself
and extension of him.

Well, I don't know
if I really thought that,
but after I almost lost
my own life, and still
spent my time trying
to piece together
who I was, I asked him,
since the literary world
knew me with my family name,
the name of my father
born in 1929,
if he was okay with me
not changing my name.

He was fine with it,
of course,
but looking back,
it makes me think
of the many ways
women have to change
who they are
to be a supplicant
to man.

And,
of course,
if we women want
to have a career,
that's fine,
but many men still think
that women should also
cook and clean
and not only birth,
but also raise their kids.

So much for us women
feeling like we can do it all
on our own, when we
are still expected
to do more work
for less pay,
and be happy
for the opportunity
in this patriarchal society.
For the oppression of women
is the underlying current
in any male-dominated culture...

wait,
who am I kidding,
it's the underlying current
in any culture.
Let's not fool ourselves.

Because I know that for years
I worked as an acquaintance rape
workshop facilitator,
which made me a counselor
and a sounding board
to more women
than I can remember,
since one in four women
are sexually assaulted
by the time they leave college,

and make that number
one in three women
over the course of their lives,
women like your sister,
your mother, your daughter —
just to name a few,
but in our society
all women have been raped,
when men rape women
with their eyes,
their laws, and their codes.*

Because women have been
denied inclusion in history,
we have been denied our history,
which denies us our present,
and even a real future.

We can carefully chronicle
this history of oppression
with seclusion and exclusion.
And we can praise
the strides we've made
despite these man-made
barricades that permeate
every aspect
of our female lives,
while remembering
the strides we still
must make
against all odds.
Because — we're strong
creatures, you know,
smiling demurely
while we take care of others,
all while getting ahead ourselves.

It's a tough job,
but we've known that all along,
and we've taken it on
without batting an eyelash,
with or without eye makeup,
and whether or not
we're reminded regularly
of all we fight against
in our battles to be good,
we feel all the things
men have historically
imposed upon us.
Whether or not we're told,
all these obstacles
are always permanently burned
in the backs of our brains,
and we still seem to do well
despite those pains
you men ingrain
in us.
So just realize
that if you ever notice
how well any woman has done,
know that everything
was accomplished
despite the big bully
in the room, always
breathing over her shoulder.
For all that hot air
breathed down by man
remind us
that we can —
and will —
defeat Goliath.

* from Marilyn French's 1977 debut novel "The Women's Room"

You've Tucked us Women Away

Written 9/8, on the day of the 1916 bid to prove that women
were capable of serving as military dispatch riders,
Augusta and Adeline Van Buren arrive in Los Angeles,
after a 60-day, 5,500 mile cross-country motorcycle trip

People say
we can't play
with the big boys,
like we
don't have
the stones,
when our stones
are so much bigger,
and have been polished
over the years
because we've handled
almost everything

you think
we're not strong enough,
you think
we don't have the
endurance,
so, please,
allow me
to relieve
this unease
and please,
allow me
to give you
the belief
that these
women can do
what all the world
needs.

you've tucked
us women away
for millennia
while we took care
of you, your home,
your family
while you went out
and acted so important
and...
what you
never realized
is that we women
are important too
we've proven that
every day of our lives

you just never noticed

so, maybe it's time
for you to watch
and see
how we
can really
roar

Keep Looking Happy

Written 8/18, the 1920 day the
U.S. 19th Amendment passed,
giving women the right to vote

Women, in theory,
should feel pleased

when we win battles
for our rights.

So whatever women do,
you keep looking happy.

That's what we women
have to do, in this

eternal uphill battle.

\#

When this country
was founded,

it was land-owning
white men who voted.

Fifty years before we
women gained that right,

white men decided
that black men —

men once slaves, or
descendants of slaves,

black men once considered
three fifths of a person —

they got the right to vote
fifty years before us women.

#

I get it, I get it,
I shouldn't be so

pessimistic —

I shouldn't look
so negatively at battles

we've had to fight
so hard to win.

I shouldn't think
that our only male

options to vote for,
they decide our fate —

they make personal
choices for us women

that we had the honor
to vote for...

#

and I understand,
we've come a long way,

baby —

we women once
couldn't attend college,

even if we had
such a long history

of caring for your home,
your food, your children —

understanding finances
so much more explicitly

than you.

And yes, us women
are running for offices

while we're still
so under-represented

and we still face
that uphill climb...

so yes, we'll keep voting
(thank you for that honor)

because before you know it
we'll have made some changes

that you didn't see
coming, because really,

when we're done,
you'll see that laws

the rest of the world
agrees with, laws

that treating women
as equals —

that kind of treatment
isn't so unreasonable

after all.

Everyone is to Blame

Written 8/31, the 1888 date Mary Ann Burton was
murdered, the first known murder by
Jack the Ripper; day in 1987 Princess Diana
died in a car crash, in front of paparazzi

we struggle for our lives at our own peril

women, in history,
have had a hard history

those who have fought
hard to make it on their own
the only way they knew how —

sometimes had it worse,
until their safety was in peril,
what, for walking down the street;
what, for trying to trust a strange man

but does it matter how any
of these women are killed,
by a murderer or by paparazzi

for rich or poor, famous or hated,
we all have to watch our backs

for this violence, everyone is to blame

Kill Us for Our Beliefs

Written 7/7, the 1456 date where a retrial verdict
acquits Joan of Arc of heresy 25 years after her death

This is the cycle we live in now.
If we women are strong, if we
fight for what's right, with our
life, we can lead armies, we'll
do everything in our power, &
we can do the right thing, and
stand on the moral ground, &
it may still seem to no avail, for
they will kill us for our beliefs. It
won't matter in the here & now
what happens to us, even if the
ones who killed us later acquit
us of any wrongdoing. Women
face uphill battles every day,
but struggles do lead to change,
even if only after a lifetime of
fighting.

Vacuum of Space

Written 10/11, the 1984 date Astronaut
Kathryn D. Sullivan aboard the
Space Shuttle Challenger becomes the first
American woman to perform a spacewalk

the men kept pushing that envelope
of course, they had to be first

because when you stop holding us back
we will surprise you with the power of our minds

so on a day like today, watch me
do all that work, watch me strap in

to that bulky space suit, just to walk
in the vacuum of space, just so I,

for once, will finally feel on my own
so I no longer feel like I'm under your thumb

Judged on Looks
written 11/13, Sadie Hawkins Day

I've vaguely heard of this holiday before,
maybe in high school, where the premise
was that women asked men to dances —

because, you know, this was a ludicrous
idea, the men were the ones who were
supposed to be asking the women out.

And back in high school, I went so far as
to ask a male friend of mine to go to Prom;
we were just friends, I wasn't going to

have a "boyfriend" date, and I thought
this friend would be the most fun to hang
with in this ritualistic high school "holiday."

But I just read that the origins of this holiday
were from Al Capp's comic strip Li'l Abner,
where Sadie Hawkins was actually homely

and no one wanted to be near her —
so her father had all the single men run
out of town, and the only one she "caught"

would be forced to marry her. Now, this
popular section of a comic strip incited
future Sadie Hawkins dances, where women

were the ones who could ask men to dance.

And yes, looking back, it may seem ludicrous,
and we women may feel we have power now,

but in the same breath, it's also funny
that a silly story in a comic strip may
have helped to incite change for women.

All because a comic book woman was ugly
and wasn't married by the time she was 35.
Sorry that we're still so judged on looks,

woman, so let's just keep working past sexism,
in that uphill battle in this patriarchal society —
even when an old comic strip's a stepping stone.

Know Peace and Rise to Power
Written 11/19, the birthday of Indira Gandhi

This "Woman of the Millennium" was
the first and only female Prime Minister.

With setbacks for gaining power in India,
she started a new party, which won.

Even after ruling for years, others
said she used devious tactics to win —

High Courts ruled against her,
ousting her from her power...

but she called a state of emergency,
enacting restrictive laws to save herself.

The public was then outraged; she was
even briefly imprisoned for corruption.

So she tried her old success tricks
again, by starting another political party,

because, you see, the new Janata Party
led to the fall of India's government.

So believe it or not, Indira Gandhi's
quote unquote corruption didn't stop

people from sweeping her back into office;
and the only reason she is the second-

longest running Prime Minister of India
is because of her assassination, in her garden,

by her own bodyguards, as revenge
for attacks on the holy Amritsar shrine

in protests for India's political integrity —
and as for integrity, and Indira Gandhi

labeled as "corrupt", keep in mind
that her husband, named Gandhi,

was of no relation to Mahatma Gandhi,
but the young girl joined Mahatma Gandhi,

wearing Khadi, or natural hand-woven
clothes, to protest British-made textiles...

—

Remember that women can know peace
and still rise to power — repeatedly.

You can claim corruption, but Indira Gandhi
worked to remove mass poverty with

"clear vision, iron will and the strictest
discipline" and her administration brought

equal pay for equal work for both sexes,
now as a part of the Indian Constitution.

Indira believed that women could do all
men could, if they were given the chance...

and Indira Gandhi took that chance whenever
she could, even telling her aunt,

"Someday I am going to lead my people
to freedom just as Joan of Arc did!"

Indira Gandhi ruled a nation, won battles,
and even fought for change — not because

she was driven as a woman, but because
she was human. Indira Gandhi, called the

'greatest mass leader of the last century',
made changes for women with her clear vision,

iron will, and her strict discipline, not because
she was a woman, but... because it was right.

Remember this, and take stock in everything
you can do. Because you know you are right.

Otherwise Reigned Supreme

Written 11/8, on the 1715 birthday of the longest-serving queen
of Prussia, Elisabeth Christine of Brunswick-Wolfenbüttel-Bevern

Stuck in my head is the movie
Monty Python and the Holy Grail,
and the scene where a father
arranges a marriage for his son,
but this "prince" rejects it. For
Crown Prince Frederick of Prussia,
who in 1733 failed his attempt to
flee his father's tyrannical regime,
was ordered to marry a woman —
Elisabeth Christine, with his choice
arranged by the Austrian court
to secure influence over Prussia.

Unlike Monty Python's Holy Grail
where the prince, in being "rescued"
tried to escape his tower, this
Prussian Prince relented; but on his
wedding day he spent one hour
with his 17-year-old bride before
walking outside alone all night.
He obviously wanted to be free
of this woman — and most women,
as he never cheated on her, so
they spent most of their time apart.

Elisabeth Christine was at first
so distraught that this prince
couldn't return her affection,
but... she learned that since they
were now married, they could ask
anything of the king and remain
comfortably secure, until the king's
death — which made her Queen.
When her husband-now-king
didn't want the tedium of being king...
he just decided to let her rule.

This situation was starting to suit
her fine; they now lived separately,
and since the ceremonial court life
didn't suit him, he left that to her,
and that suited her just fine. He
could come to occasional functions,
but otherwise, Elisabeth Christine
reigned supreme, just how she liked it.
Because during the Seven Years' War
he remained absent, while she was
the symbol of Prussian resilience.

During her reign she authored several
works (some based on the passing
of loved ones) that were included
in the library of the king; this woman
also gave more than half her income
to charity. Prussia's Elisabeth Christine,
their longest-serving queen, found out
how to take a situation no one wanted,
and turn it into a life where a woman
could make a real difference — which
is what we women do to this day.

Vaulted to Silhouette the Sky

Written 12/23, the 583 date the Maya queen
Yohl Ik'nal is crowned ruler of Palenque

I gave birth
to the greatest leaders
of our time

I was also the
first female ruler in Mayan
history, and

was only one
of a very few female rulers
known from Maya —

that was borne
with a royal title. But I'm sure
you haven't heard

of me or what
I have done, because, really,
why would you

think a woman
could do anything, amount
to anything, or

rule anything,
even if a woman earned it.
Tombs vaulted

to me adorned
the silhouette of the sky;
I'll be sculpted

in the vaults
of my offspring, more leaders
you'll forget...

because, how
could you — Why would you
even remember

something you
were never taught. Your now
patriarchy

shuns women
being in any power, so you'll
brush me

under your
proverbial rug. Just know that
despite your

efforts, women
can be in power, despite your
efforts to the

otherwise.
Because when we come,
we'll rule

in a way you
never expected. Because you
never learned...

because they
didn't teach you. Or you chose
to not listen.

Veins Burn Blue with Greatness

Written 10/29, on the birthday in 1825 of the
last Queen of Romania, Marie Alexandra Victoria

I knew I was destined for greatness,
I knew royalty coursed through these blue veins,
my strength was great, even when
my royal family wanted me to marry my cousin —
my own cousin. I refused the proposal,
I don't care if he would be the future King George V.
You see, that's what family does,
and that's what royalty does, they choose your life
for you, which is why I was bound
to Crown Prince Ferdinand of Romania. ...If they think
they can make all of my choices for me...
then just try. For what they don't understand is that
I am the one with the power.
I will wield true influence over my weak-minded husband,
even before I stepped into my throne.
I am the one who made crucial decisions during WWI
that gained us more land and power,
all while my loyal subjects still adored me. I did all this
while writing stories in books to shock
the royal family — which may be why my subjects still
revered me, even as a model patriot.
For you see, even when those who think they know
better try to hold you back, when
you know you are destined for greatness, you can
defy them. And you can still win.

Voluptuous, and Intelligent Too

about Chicago Tribune news reporter Maurine Dallas Watkins, who,
after reporting about female murderers who dressed up, wore make-up,
styled their hair, and acted "feminine" to get out of murder convictions,
then wrote a play on it, which was later adapted into the musical "Chicago"

Too many times
men treated me
as if I couldn't have a brain,
and they objectified
me every chance
they could take.

I was thrown into their
male-dominated den, but I learned fast —
I had the brains,
but I could also use what made men

weak. You see, I wore mini skirts,
plunging necklines and padded bras,
and I learned
how to flip my hair and act ignorant,

because — get a load of this —
being intelligent doesn't work
with men's notion
of objectification.
I played my part,

I was adored
(and my men actually
thought I was a natural blonde)
and I knew exactly how to play their game —

because I could flaunt my wares
just enough to make men salivate,
I allowed men to adore,
until I could show them a thing or two
about being intelligent too.

Emphatic One
Written 9/23, Equal Pay Day

After working so hard
and doing so well at work
I couldn't take my low pay anymore

I knew it was wrong
I knew it wasn't fair
and I had to do something about it

I took a deep breath,
set up a meeting with my boss —
the owner of the company

I don't think he knew
what this meeting was really about,
so I started my speech

no, wait, it wasn't a speech
it was more like a conversation,
an emphatic one at that

and when I explained
that at this company
I do the work of two people

I think he thought I was going to ask
for double pay (and really, I didn't
make much, but I didn't want

to lose my job over asking for a raise)
but after I talked,
after I reasoned, and
after he may have realized

that he had nobody else that could do
all this work by the deadlines,
and do it well, that he knew, suddenly,

paying me reasonably, seemed...
reasonable. But uphill battles
for us woman are the norm...

You may want to think
that if women work hard,
women would earn

the pay they deserve,
but here's the newsflash,
we women work harder

than men for less than
equal pay, and shouldn't we be
happy we've even got jobs?

I mean, what are these women
complaining about when they're
supposed to take care of the house

and raise babies for men anyway
(and don't forget, that's after
taking the man's name too,

because women can claim
nothing for themselves anymore).
Because the one thing I learned

is to take the reigns and win
every battle, only so women
can be treated as equals.

It's just a shame that each woman
has to take this fight on, because
just because one woman does well,

that doesn't mean all of mankind
(yes, you heard me, "man"kind)
will make the connection

that rights for one woman
might actually mean
rights for all women. So...

I know it's an uphill battle,
but I just want you to remember
that I'm always in your corner.

Driving By His House

I know it's pretty pathetic of me, I don't know what I'm trying to prove. I don't even want to see him again. I don't want to have to think about him, I don't want to think about his big eyebrows or the fact that he hunched over a little when he walked or that he hurt me so much.

I know it's pretty pathetic of me, but sometimes when I'm driving, I'll take a little detour and drive by his house. I'll just drive by, I won't slow down, I won't stop by, I won't say hello, I won't beat his head in, I won't even cry. I'll just drive by, see a few cars in the driveway, see no signs of life through the windows, and then I'll just keep driving.

I don't know why I do it. He never sees me, and I never see him, although I thought I didn't want to see him anyway. When I first met him I wasn't afraid of him. Now I'm so afraid that I have to drive by his house every once in a while, just to remind myself of the fear. We all like the taste of fear, you know, the thought that there's something out there stronger than us. The thought that there's something out there we can beat, even if we have to fight to the death.

But that can't be it, no, it just can't be, I don't like this fear, I don't like it. I don't want to drive by, I want to be able to just go on with my life, to not think about it. I want to be strong again. I want to be strong.

So today I did it again, I haven't done it for a while, drive by his house, but I did it again today. When I turned on to his street, I put on my sunglasses so that in case he saw me he couldn't tell that I was looking. And then I picked up my car phone and acted like I was talking to someone.

And I drove by, holding my car phone, talking to my imaginary friend, trying to unobviously glance at the house on my left. There's a lamppost at the end of his driveway. I always noticed it, the lampshade was a huge glass ball, I always thought it was ugly. This time three cars were there. One of those could have been his. Through the front window, no people, no lights. I drive around a corner, take a turn and get back on the road I was supposed to be on.

One day, when I'm driving by and I get that feeling again, that feeling like death, well then, I just might do it again.

20150115 8:36PM CST

While in India John said to me, "So you know, all the horn honks are not for you..." (because usually at home whenever I'd go for a walk along the streets I'd usually get at least one horn honking, if not a cat call from an open window, because men are often base and sexually rude that way), and I laughed and said I knew that, everyone honks at everything here because people cram into any spaces and do not use lanes or stop signs, I get it. But not fifteen seconds after he said that to me, that the horn honks are not for me, I sensed someone walking behind us. I signaled to John to move to the side so they could pass (because as a woman, being followed is usually not a good thing, because anything could be a threat).

But just after he made this comment about horn honks for me, and just after I let someone walking behind us pass us, then we both watched the man (probably all 5' 2" of him), even after he was in front of us, repeatedly turn around to look at me specifically. He'd look back to where he was walking, and then he'd turn around again, look at me for a second or two, then turn back to watch where he was walking.

He did this at least six times, until we got off that road.

Well, it's nice to see that sexism and men degrading women is global.

Unmarried Women and Dead Bodies Everywhere

the Ganges River in India,
the most sacred river to Hindus
is still religiously renowned

but on one day not too long ago,
at one tributary of the Ganges river
they discovered twenty-eight bodies

the locals first spotted the corpses
when vultures surrounded those bodies
as they piled up along the shore

online news sources explain
that bodies may have been left there
when families couldn't afford a burial

and at those same online news sources,
lucky you, you can see videos of dogs
eating at the flesh of the dead

—

but I was there, I read those newspapers
as the Star of India came to me daily,
while locals discovered more bodies:

before they found one hundred and four
the local papers explained
that this 'tradition' of "jalpravah"

is a custom in some cultures —

when unmarried women die
their bodies are dumped in the river

—

unrecognizably decomposed,
more and more bodies
of unmarried women

kept floating to the surface
in just a few days,
in the sacred Ganges river

—

I kept looking for an explanation,
and all I could think was that
this river was supposed to be sacred

and I wondered if this is their effort
to give these women a family
in the afterlife, putting them in a river

they call sacred

because I know how they view women
in India, cover their skin, they don't talk back,
because even though women

are treated like nothing by men there,
they'd be less than nothing
if they're not married

हर जगह अविवाहित महिलाएं और लाशें

भारत में गंगा नदी,
हिंदुओं के लिए सबसे पवित्र नदी
अभी भी धार्मिक रूप से प्रसिद्ध है

लेकिन एक दिन बहुत पहले नहीं,
गंगा नदी की एक सहायक नदी पर
उन्होंने अट्ठाईस निकायों की खोज की

स्थानीय लोगों ने सबसे पहले लाशों को देखा
जब गिद्धों ने उन शवों को घेर लिया
जैसे ही वे किनारे पर ढेर हो गए

ऑनलाइन समाचार स्रोत बताते हैं
हो सकता है कि शव वहाँ छोड़े गए हों
जब परिवार दफन नहीं कर सकते थे

और उन्हीं ऑनलाइन समाचार स्रोतों पर,
आप भाग्यशाली हैं, आप कुत्तों के वीडियो देख सकते हैं
मरे हुओं का मांस खाकर

-

लेकिन मैं वहां था, मैंने उन अखबारों को पढ़ा
जैसा कि टाइम्स ऑफ इंडिया रोज मेरे पास आता था,
जबकि स्थानीय लोगों ने और शवों की खोज की:

एक सौ चार मिलने से पहले
स्थानीय कागजात समझाया
कि "जलप्रवाह" की यह 'परंपरा'

कुछ संस्कृतियों में एक प्रथा है -

जब अविवाहित महिलाओं की मृत्यु हो जाती है
उनके शवों को नदी में फेंक दिया जाता है

-

अपरिचित रूप से विघटित,
अधिक से अधिक शरीर
अविवाहित महिलाओं की

सतह पर तैरता रहा
कुछ ही दिनों में,
पवित्र गंगा नदी में

-

मैं स्पष्टीकरण ढूंढता रहा,
और मैं बस यही सोच सकता था कि
इस नदी को पवित्र माना जाता था

और मुझे आश्चर्य हुआ कि क्या यह उनका प्रयास है
इन महिलाओं को देने के लिए

The Burning

I take the final swig of vodka
feel it burn its way down my throat
hiss at it scorching my tongue
and reach for the bottle to pour myself another.
I think of how my tonsils scream
every time I let the alcohol rape me.
Then I look down at my hands —
shaking — holding the glass of poison —
and think of how these were the hands
that should have pushed you away from me.
But didn't. And I keep wondering
why I took your hell, took your poison.
I remember how you burned your way
through me. You corrupted me
from the inside out, and I kept coming back.
I let you infect me, and now you've
burned a hole through me. I hated it.
Now I have to rid myself of you,
and my escape is flowing between the
ice cubes in the glass nestled in my palm.
But I have to drink more. The burning
doesn't last as long as you do.

het verbranden

Ik nam de laatste slok vodka
voelde hoe het brandde in mijn keel
het verschroeide mijn tong
en greep naar de fles om mezelf te trakteren
Ik dacht er aan hoe mijn slokdarm schreeuwde
telkens ik de alkohol me liet verkrachten.
Dan keek ik hoe mijn handen -
beefde - met het glas vergif in mijn hand-
en denken dat het de handen van een ander waren
die je van me moeten wegduwen.
Maar ik deed het niet. Me afvragend
waarom ik met jou door de hel liep, je vergif nam
Ik herinnerde me hoe je een weg brandde
door mij . Je chanteerde mijn ziel, en ik bleef komen
Ik liet je me verzieken , en nu heb je
een groot gat in mij. Ik haat het.
Nu moet ik mezelf en jou redden,
mijn vlucht is tussen de ijsblokjes
die zich nestelden in de palm van mijn hand.
Maar ik moet meer drinken. Het branden
duurt niet zolang als jou left

All Men Have Secrets

all men have secrets and here is mine.
Strength is my weakness
and now my shoulders don't stay in place.
You ask me to open my eyes
but they are. At least I think they are.
Why don't you take me in your arms?
Why don't you seduce me?
Tear me in half. Rip me apart.
Just don't cast me aside.
I don't want to be strong. Be strong
for me, so that I can adjust my chin
and not have to worry about
whether or not my eyes are open.

iedereen heeft geheimen

iedereen heeft geheimen en dit is het mijne.
Kracht is mijn zwakke plek
en nu blijven mijn schouders niet op hun plaats.
Je vroeg me mijn ogen te openen
maar ze zijn open, dat denk ik toch.
Waarom neem je me niet in jou armen ?
Waarom verleid je me niet ?
Trek me uiteen. Scheur me in stukken.
Hou geen rekening met mijn kuisheid
Ik wil niet sterk zijn . wees sterk voor mij,
zodat ik me kan laten gaan
en nergens zorgen over te maken
of mijn ogen nu open zijn of niet.

I Wanted Pain

You screamed at me to pull over.
You wanted me to stop.
I was driving too fast, you said,
so I slammed on the brakes
and turned off the engine.
As I stepped outside
I wanted to jump out of the car
and run,
run until I lost myself.
And yet I wanted to fall.
I wanted to fall to the ground.
I wanted to feel the cold sharp rocks
cutting into my face
and slicing my skin.
I wanted pain to feel good again.
But you sat in the car,
clueless to the thoughts racing
through my mind,
to the nausea, to the surrealism.
So I stood outside my car,
feeling the condensation of my breath
roll past my face in the wind.
It was a constant, nagging reminder
that I still had to breathe.

Ik verlangde naar pijn

Je schreeuwde naar mij aan de kant te gaan.
Je wou dat ik stopte.
Ik reed te hard, zei je,
daarom stampte ik op de remmen
en zette de motor af.
Ik wou uit de auto springen
en weglopen,
lopen tot ik mezelf verloor.
Ja ik wou vallen.
Ik wou op de grond vallen
Ik wou de kille scherpe grint voelen
die in mijn gezicht sneden
en mijn kin openhaalde.
Ik wou pijn om me weer goed te voelen.
Maar jij zat nog in je auto,
klaar om te racen
mijn geest aan te porren,
tot waanzinnigheid , boven alle grenzen heen.
Ik stond geleund tegen mijn auto,
voelde mijn verzwakte adem
mijn krullen vlogen door de wind tegen mijn gelaat
Ik moest me concentreren op mijn adem
de uitdaging in jou macht te geraken negeren
zolang ik ademen en denken kon.

the Martyr and the Saint

they gave their daughter the name
of the Patron Saint of television

and the television's always been
one thing she hated about him

or was it the drinking that he needed
more than her

the business has gone bad
I'm a failure I'm not a man

he said he respected her
then he'd call her

a twenty-dollar whore from Vegas

and the mother would hold
the child, the saint, the pure angel

hold her ears and hope she
couldn't hear

de martelaar en de heilige

Ze gaven hun dochter de naam
van de patroon van de televisie

en de televisie was iets
dat ze altijd haatte bij hem

of was het dat drinken dat hij nodig had
meer dan hij haar nodig had

de zaken gingen slecht
ik ben een mislukkeling ik ben geen man

hij zei haar te respecteren
dan belde hij haar

voor twintig dollar gewonnen in Vegas

en de moeder wou het kind,
de heilige, de echte engel

hield haar oor
in de hoop iets te kunnen opvangen

White Knuckled

The hot air was sticking
to her skin   almost pulling
tugging at her very
flesh   as she walked
outside   down the
stairs from the train
station. Just then a
breeze hot and
sticky   hit her
in just the wrong
way, brushed against her
lower neck, and she
felt his breath again,
not his breath
when he raped
her, but his   stench
hot   rank
when he was
just close to her.

Her breath quickened,
like the catch of her
breath when she has
just stopped
crying. All the emotion
is still there   not
going away.   She
walks to the bottom
of the stairs, railing
white-knuckled by her
small tender hands,
the hands of a child,
and that ninety degree
breeze suddenly
gives her a
chill. They say when
you get a chill it means
a goose walked
over your grave.
She knows better. She knows
that it is him
walking, and that
he trapped that child
in that grave

biele hánky

Horúci vzduch sa lepil
na jej kožu   takmer ťahajúc
šklbajúc jej
mäsom,   keď prechádzala
von   dolu schodmi
z vlakovej
stanice. Vtedy
ju udrel horúci a lepkavý
vánok
tým nesprávnym spôsobom
zavadil   o jej
šiju a ona
znovu cítila jeho dych,
nie jeho dych
keď ju znásilnil,
ale jeho   zápach
horúci   odporný
keď bol
už blízko pri nej.

Jej dych zrýchlil,
ako keď chytila
dych, po tom čo
prestala
plakať. Všetky emócie
sú tam stále,
nejdú preč. Prejde na
spodok
schodov, zábradlie
s bielymi hánkami jej
malých nežných rúk,
rúk dieťaťa,
a ten tridsaťdva stupňový
vánok jej rozbehá po tele
zimomriavky.
Hovorí sa, že keď
máte zimomriavky znamená to
že hus prešla
ponad váš hrob.
Ona to vie lepšie. Ona vie
že to je jeho
chôdza, a že on
uväznil, to dieťa v
tom hrobe.

Women's Very Existence

rape is neither a sex crime
or a crime of passion
rape is not an isolated brutal crime
against women
it is an attack by men
on women's bodies
on women's feelings
on women's very existence
Bob Lamm, 1976

i still have to take showers a lot. i mean,
every once in a while, no matter how clean
i am to the rest of the world, i have to go
take a shower. i lock all the doors, i close
the shades on the windows, i put a towel
over the bathroom mirror. turn the water on,
piping hot, so steam is billowing out of
the bath tub. i finally undress, open the
curtain, put my foot in, burn my foot with
the water. i wish i could hold my foot there,
just a little longer. i turn down the water.
wait for it to cool down, then step in. then
i just put my head under the shower head. hold
it there for a while. catch my breath. get the
soap. start scrubbing. i use the soap first,
then i get the bath brush. scrub off a layer
of skin. i know this makes no sense. my skin
is red, from the heat, from the scrubbing.
but i know i'm still not getting it off, it's
down there, the molecules are embedded
deep inside of me, and i'll have to rip my skin
off, pull out my organs before it goes away.
but for now all i can do is take showers.

Podstata ženského bytia

znásilnenie nie je ani sexuálna zločin
ani zločin z vášne
znásilnenie nie je izolovaný brutálny zločin
páchaný na ženách
to je útok mužov
na ženské telá
na ženské pocity
na podstatu ženského bytia
Bob Lamm, 1976

stále sa veľa sprchujem. mám na mysli,
raz za čas sa musím ísť
osprchovať bez ohľadu na to, ako čisto vyzerám
pre zvyšok sveta. zamknem všetky dvere, stiahnem žalúzie,
prehodím uterák cez zrkadlo v kúpeľni.
pustím vodu
vriacu, tak že sa nad vaňou vznáša para. konečne sa
vyzlečiem, odtiahnem
záves, vložím dnu nohu, vodou si popálim
chodidlo. kiež by som tam mohla podržať nohu
len o niečo dlhšie. stiahnem vodu.
počkám kým vychladne, potom vkročím dnu
potom si dám hlavu pod hlavicu sprchy. držím si ju tam
na chvíľu. zatajím dych. zoberiem
mydlo. začnem sa drhnúť. mydlo použijem prvé,
potom si vezmem kúpeľovú kefu. zoškrabem si vrstvu
kože. viem, že to nedáva zmysel. moja koža
je červená, z tepla, z drhnutia.
ale ja viem, že som to stále nedala preč, je to
tam dole, molekuly sú zapustené
hlboko v mojom vnútri, a ja si budem musieť roztrhať svoju
kožu, vytiahnuť z tela orgány pred tým, než to zmizne.
ale nateraz všetko, čo pre to môžem urobiť, je sprchovať sa.

part of the poem **Right There, By Your Heart**

II

have you ever had that feeling before, you
know, the one when someone is telling
you something you don't want to hear, like
if someone was about to tell you that someone
died and you knew what they were going to say
and you still didn't want to hear it, or if
someone did something to you didn't like,
like when you were little and the kids at the
bus stop shot pebbles and spit balls at you every
day because you were smart and you still had
to go to the bus stop every morning and just
try to ignore them? and when that happens
it feels like a medium sized rock just fell
into the bottom of your stomach, and you
don't want to move because you're afraid
that the rock will hurt the inside of your stomach
and so you just have to sit there and hope
the rock goes away? or else you get the feeling
in your chest, right between your lungs, it feels
like someone is pressing against the bone there,
right there by your heart, and you've got to
breathe, you're not going to be able to take
that pressure, that force any longer?

VI

i don't know how many times the idea of seeing him
went through my mind. at least once a week i'd imagine
a scene where he'd confront me, and i'd somehow
be able to fight him back, to show him that he didn't
bother me anymore, to show him that the rock wasn't
there anymore. to somehow be able to prove that
i wasn't a victim any more. i was a survivor. that's
what they call it now, you see, survivor, because
victim sounds too trying for someone who has been
raped. so i keep saying i'm over it but i keep imagining
mark all over again, not raping me, but following me
on the street, coming to my door with flowers, or
sending me a valentine. but once, when i saw him
walking out of a record store as i was walking in, the
rock fell so hard that i thought i was going to be sick
right there by the cash register, right there by those
metal things at the doorway that beep when you
try to take merchandise out of the store, you know
what those things are, i just can't think of what
they're called. but if i did that, then he'd know he was still
winning, to this day. how many years has it been? how
many years since he did that to me? how many years
since i've been wanting to fight him, since i've been
feeling that rock in my god-damned stomach?
i managed to hide my face from him in the store so he
didn't see me as he walked out. when i saw he was
gone, i wondered why i still felt the pressure in my
chest. i thought the pressure was going to turn
my body inside-out. i reached for my heart, grabbed
at my shirt. maybe the pain was always there, right there,
by my heart, but i try not to think of it until i
go through times like those.

Časť básne Práve Tam, pri Tvojom srdci

II

už ste niekedy mali ten pocit, viete, ten,
keď vám niekto hovorí to čo nechcete počuť,
ako keď sa vám niekto chystá povedať, že niekto
umrel a vy viete, čo vám chce povedať
ale aj tak to nechcete počuť, alebo ak vám
niekto urobil niečo, čo sa vám nepáčilo,
ako keď ste boli malý a deti na
autobusovej zastávke na vás každý deň strieľali
kamienky a pľuvali cez fľusátko, len preto
že ste boli múdry a aj tak ste stále každé ráno museli
ísť na autobusovú zastávku a
pokúsiť sa ignorovať ich? a keď sa to stane
máte pocit akoby vám stredne veľký kameň spadol
do spodnej časti žalúdka a vy sa nechcete
ani pohnúť, pretože sa bojíte
že vám skala poraní vnútro žalúdka
a tak vám neostáva nič iné len sedieť a dúfať,
že skala zmizne? lebo inak budete mať ten pocit
v hrudi, priamo medzi vašimi pľúcami, je to
ako keď vám niekto tlačí na hrudnú kosť,
hneď tam pri vašom srdci, a vy musíte
dýchať, nebudete schopný zvládať ten
tlak, tú silu dlhšie?

VI

neviem, koľkokrát mi preletela mysľou myšlienka toho že ho
vidím. aspoň raz týždenne som si predstavovala,
scénu, kde by mi stál zoči-voči, a ja by som nejako
bola schopná bojovať s ním, aby som mu ukázala, že už ma
netrápi, aby som mu ukázala že kameň zmizol.
byť tak nejakým spôsobom schopná dokázať mu, že už viac nie
som obeťou. že som prežila. To je
to, čo hovoria, ako to teraz nazývajú, prežila, pretože
obeť znie príliš vyčerpávajúco pre niekoho, kto bol
znásilnený. a tak si dookola hovorím, je to za mnou, ale aj tak si
úplne znova predstavujem marka, nie ako ma znásilňuje, ale ako
ma nasleduje po ulici, prichádza k mojim dverám s kvetinami,
alebo ako mi posiela valentínku. ale raz, keď som ho videla ako
vychádza z obchodu s cd-čkami, ako som vchádzala dnu,
kameň dopadol tak tvrdo, že som si myslela že mi bude zle
hneď tam pri pokladni, tam pri tých kovových predmetoch pri
dverách, ktoré pípnu, keď sa niekto pokúsi vziať tovar z
obchodu, viete, čo sú to za veci,
ja si proste nemôžem spomenúť na to, ako
sa volajú. ale keby som to urobila, vedel by, že do dnešného dňa
je víťazom. koľko rokov tomu bolo? koľko
je to rokov, ako si mi to urobil? koľko je tomu rokov
ako chcem proti nemu bojovať, odkedy cítim ten
prekliaty kameň v žalúdku? keď vychádzal, podarilo sa mi pred
ním skryť svoju tvár v obchode tak, aby ma nevidel. keď som
videla, že je preč, divila som sa, prečo ešte stále cítim tlak v
hrudi. myslela som, že ten tlak obráti
moje telo naruby. siahla som si na srdce, schmatla
sa za košeľu. možno že bolesť tam vždy bola, práve tam,
pri mojom srdci, ale snažím sa nemyslieť na to, až kým
neprejdem niečím ako toto.

What the Hell is She Complaining About

i can't go around telling people
about what you did to me
you see, nobody wants to hear it
and nobody wants to hear a girl whining
what the hell's she complaining about anyway?
but you know, nobody knows
the effects of what you've done
nobody knows that I showered for weeks
no, months
to try to feel clean after you did that to me
nobody knows why i have
violent fits of rage
how I'd hit the wall, rip up the plaster

you want to know what i think of men now?
you want to know their place in my life now?
you see, i didn't know what else to do
so i became the rapist
and now i let men do nice things for me
but i always keep them at a safe distance
i never let them get too close
because i don't care how nice you are
i'll always keep you at arm's length
i learned my lesson

so yeah, you had an effect on me
and i have to bottle it all up
because no one wants to hear the details
i mean, i wasn't physically injured
what the hell could i be complaining about anyway?

but you know, there are times
when i wish you left a mark,
like a bee sting or something,
so people could see a welt
from what you had done

wait, no, i take that back
i'd wish i was stung by a bee
and i was allergic to bees

because then my blood pressure would drop,
my pulse would get rapid,
i'd fall into anaphylactic shock
my skin would turn white
before I got the hospital
as they tried to keep me alive

all because of a bee sting

while everyone else is thinking,
a bee sting,
what the hell is she complaining about

Na čo sa do pekla sťažuje

nemôžem ísť dookola a rozprávať ľudom
o tom, čo si mi urobil
chápeš, nikto to nechce počuť
a nikto nechce počuť fňukajúce dievča
na čo sa do pekla vlastne sťažuje?
ale ty to vieš, nikto nevie
o následkoch toho, čo si urobil
nikto nevie, že som sa sprchovala týždne
nie, mesiace
pokúšala sa cítiť čistá potom čo si mi urobil,
nikto nevie, prečo mávam
násilné záchvaty hnevu
ako som udrela do steny, vytrhala omietku

chceš vedieť, čosi teraz myslím o mužoch?
chceš vedieť aké miesto majú teraz v mojom živote?
v--ieš, nevedela som, čo iné som mala urobiť
tak som sa stala násilníkom
a teraz dovolím robiť mužom pre mňa pekné veci
nikdy si ich nepripustím príliš blízko
pretože ma nezaujíma akí ste milí
vždy si Vás budem držať od tela
poučila som sa

takže hej, mal si na mňa vplyv
a ja to všetko musím potlačiť
pretože nikto nechce počuť podrobnosti
chcem tým povedať, nebola som fyzicky zranená
na čo sa do pekla by som sa vlastne sťažovala?
ale vždy si ich držím v bezpečnej vzdialenosti
ale viete, sú časy,
keď si želám aby si na mne zanechal stopu,
ako včelie bodnutie alebo také niečo,
aby ľudia mohli vidieť ranku
spôsobenú tým, čo si urobil

počkaj, nie, beriem to späť
želám si, aby som bola pichnutá včelou
a bola alergická na včely

pretože potom by mi klesol krvný tlak,
môj pulz by sa zrýchlil,
a upadla by som do anafylaktického šoku
moja koža by zbledla
predtým ako by som sa dostala do nemocnice
ako by sa snažili udržať ma nažive

všetko kvôli včeliemu bodnutiu

zatiaľ čo všetci ostatní si myslia,
včelie bodnutie,
Na čo sa do pekla sťažuje

Burn It In

Once I was at a beach
off the west coast of Florida
it was New Year's eve
and the yellow moon hung over the gulf
like a swaying lantern.
And I was watching the waves crash in front of me
with a friend
and the wind picked up
and my friend just stared at that moon for a while
and then closed his eyes.
I asked him what he was thinking.
He said, "I wanted to look at this scene,
and memorize it, burn it into my brain,
record it in my mind, so I can call it up when I want to.
So I can have it with me always."

I too have my recorders.
I burn these things into my brain,
I burn these things onto pages.
I pick and choose what needs to be said,
what needs to be remembered.

When I first went to college
I was studying to be a computer science
engineer, I wanted to make a lot of money
I wanted to beat everyone else
because burned in my brain were the taunts
of kids who were in cliques
so others could do the thinking for them
because burned in my brain were the evenings
of the high school dances I never went to
because burned in my brain were the people
I knew I was better than
who thought they were better than me.
Well, yes, I wanted to make a lot of money
I wanted to beat everyone else
but I hated what I was doing

I hated what I saw around me
hated all the pain people put each other through
and all of these memories just kept flooding me
so in my spare time
to keep me sane, to keep me alive
I wrote down the things I could not say
that was how I recorded things.

When I looked around me, and saw friends
raping my friends
I wrote, I burned into these nightmares with a pen
and yes, I have this recorded
I have all of this recorded.

What did you think I was doing
when I was stuffing hand-written notes into my pockets
or typing long hours into the night?
In my spare time, I was sitting in the corner of a cafe
scribbling into my notebook.
I was sitting in the computer lab
slamming my hands, my fingers against the keyboard
because there were too many atrocities in the world
too many injustices that I had witnessed
too many people who had wronged me

and I had a lot of work to do.
There had to be a record of what you've done.

Did you think your crimes would go unpunished?
And did you think that you could come back, years later,
slap me on the back with a friendly hello
and think I wouldn't remember?
You see, that's what I have my poems for
so there will always be a record
of what you have done
I have defiled many pages
in your honor, you who swung
your battle ax high above your head
and thought no one would remember in the end.
Well, I made a point to remember.

Yes, I have defiled many pages
and have you defiled many women?
You, the man who rapes my friends?
You, the man who rapes my sisters?
You, the man who rapes me?
Is this what makes you a strong man?

you want to know why I do the things I do

I had to record these things
that is what kept me together
when people were dying
that is what kept me together
when my friends went off to war
that is what kept me together
when my friends were raped
and left for dead
that is what kept me together
when no one bothered to notice this
or change this
or care about this
these recordings kept me together

I need to record these things
to remind myself
of where I came from
I need to record these things
to remind myself
that there are things to value
and things to hate
I need to record these things
to remind myself
that there are things worth fighting for
worth dying for
I need to record these things
to remind myself
that I am alive

Vypáľ to

Raz som bola na pláži
na západnom pobreží Floridy
bolo to na Silvestra
a žltý mesiac visel nad zálivom
ako kymácajúci sa lampión.
A ja som sa s kamarátom dívala
na narážajúce vlny predo mnou
a zdvihol sa vietor
a môj kamarát len chvíľu uprene pozeral na ten mesiac
a potom zavrel oči.
Spýtala som sa ho, čo si myslí.
Povedal: „Chcel som sa pozerať na túto scénu,
a zapamätať si ju, vyryť si ju do pamäti,
zaznamenať si ju v mojej mysli,
a tak si ju môžem vyvolať, kedy chcem.
Takže ju môžem mať vždy so sebou. "

Aj ja mám svoje diktafóny.
Vypaľujem si tieto veci do mozgu,
Vypaľujem tieto veci na stránky.
Vyberiem a zvolím, čo je potrebné povedať,
čo má ostať zapamätané.

Keď som šla prvýkrát na Univerzitu
študovala som za inžinierku
počítačovej vedy, chcela som zarobiť veľa peňazí
chcela som sa poraziť všetkých ostatných
pretože vypálené v mojom mozgu boli posmešky
detí, ktoré boli v partiách
aby za nich mohli myslieť ostatní
pretože vypálené v mojom mozgu boli večery
stredoškolských tancov na ktoré som nikdy nechodila
pretože vypálení v mojom mozgu boli ľudia

od ktorých som bola lepšia
ktorí si mysleli, že boli lepší ako ja.
Nuž, áno, chcela som zarobiť veľa peňazí
Chcela som poraziť všetkých ostatných
ale nenávidela som, čo som robila
Nenávidela som, čo som videla okolo seba
nenávidela som všetku tú bolesť ktorú si ľudia navzájom
spôsobovali a všetky tie spomienky ma stále zaplavujú

a tak vo svojom voľnom čase,
aby som sa nezbláznila, aby som ostala na žive
napísala som si veci o ktorých som nemohla hovoriť,
takto som si zaznamenávala veci.
Keď som sa pozrela okolo seba a videla priateľov
znásilňovať priateľov
Písala som, spálila som tieto nočné mory perom
a áno, mám to nahrané
Mám to všetko nahrané.
Čo si myslíte, že som robila
keď som si pchala rukami písané poznámky do vreciek
alebo písala dlhé hodiny do noci?
Vo svojom voľnom čase, som sedela v rohu kaviarne
čmárala si do môjho zošita.
Sedela som v počítačovej učebni
udierajúc rukami, prstami do klávesnice
pretože na svete bolo príliš veľa zverstiev
príliš veľa nespravodlivosti, ktorej som bola svedkom
príliš veľa ľudí, ktorí mi ublížili

a ja som mala veľa práce.
Musel byť záznam o tom, čo ste urobili.

Mysleli ste si, že Vaše zločiny zostanú nepotrestané?
A mysleli ste si, že o pár rokov sa môžete vrátiť späť,
potľapkať ma po chrbte s priateľským ahoj
a myslieť si, že si to nebudem pamätať?
Vidíte, na toto mám moje básne
takže vždy bude záznam o
tom, čo ste urobili
Poškvrnila som veľa strán
na vašu počesť, vy, ktorý ste mávali

bojovou sekerou vysoko nad hlavou
a mysleli si že na konci si to nikto nebude pamätať
No, predsavzala som si aby sa nezabudlo.
Áno, poškvrnila som veľa strán
poškvrnili ste mnoho žien?
Ty, muž, ktorý znásilňuje mojich priateľov?
Ty, muž, ktorý znásilňuje moje sestry?
Ty, muž, ktorý znásilňuje mňa?
Je toto to, čo z Teba robí silného muža?

Chcete vedieť, prečo robím veci, ktoré robím

Musela som si zaznamenať tieto veci
to je to, čo ma držalo pokope
keď ľudia zomierali
to je to, čo ma držalo pokope
keď moji priatelia odchádzali do vojny
to je to, čo ma držalo pokope
keď mojich priateľov znásilnili
a odišli na večnosť
to je to, čo ma držalo pokope
keď sa nikto neobťažoval s tým aby si to všimol
alebo to zmenil
alebo sa o to staral
tieto záznamy ma stále držali pokope
Musím si zaznamenať tieto veci
aby som si pripomenula
odkiaľ som prišla
Musím si zaznamenať tieto veci
aby som si pripomenula
že existujú veci, ktoré si treba vážiť
a veci ktoré treba nenávidieť
Musím si zaznamenať tieto veci
aby som si pripomenula
že existujú veci, za ktoré sa oplatí bojovať
stojí za ne zomrieť
Musím si zaznamenať tieto veci
aby som si pripomenula
že som nažive

Domestic Violence in America, Nashville, Tennessee (nose)

i have had my cheek bone
and nose reconstructed twice

we're divorced now
but he still keeps calling me

he keeps denying it in court

**domáce násilie v Amerike,
Nashville, Tennessee (nos)**

mala som dvakrát prerábanú
lícnu kosť a nos

už sme rozvedený
ale neustále mi volá

stále to popiera na súde

Domestic Violence in America,
Nashville, Tennessee (stick)

according to accounts, her husband
allegedly locked her and their
four-year-old son in their house

for about forty hours. They were
essentially hostages. The husband
then allegedly beat the woman

while the son watched. This is the
stick he allegedly used to keep her
in line, it looks like a metal broom

or mop handle, it's hollow, and you
see, here is a bend in it from the
hitting. The bend looks like a twist

of a garden hose. And this bloody
knit glove, it was tied on here, at
the end of the stick, so that when he

allegedly hit her it didn't scar her.
Isn't that funny? You can tell that
the son was there for it all, too, he

doesn't talk much at all, and he never
leaves his mother's side. She limps down
the hallway now, and he follows.

**domáce násilie v Amerike,
Nashville, Tennessee (palica)**

podľa správy, ju jej manžel údajne
zamkol spolu s ich štvorročným
synom v ich dome na

asi štyridsať hodín. Boli
v podstate rukojemníkmi. Manžel
potom údajne zbil ženu

zatiaľ čo sa syn pozeral. Je to
palica ktorú údajne použil aby ju udržal
v pozore, vyzerá ako kovová metla

alebo rukoväť mopu, je dutá, a môžete
vidieť, že tu je ohnutá od
bitia. Ohyb vyzerá ako spletená

záhradná hadica. A táto krvavá
pletená rukavica, bola priviazaná tu, na
konci tyče, takže keď ju

údajne udrel, nezanechalo jej to jazvu.
Nie je to srandovné? Je vidieť, že
syn tam tiež bol po celý ten čas,

nerozpráva veľmi veľa, a nikdy sa nepohne
od matky. Teraz kríva dolu chodbou, a on ju
nasleduje.

Thank You, Women who Work I

Thank you, women who work
In this way you make
an indispensable contribution
to the growth of a culture
which unites reason and feeling,
to a model of life ever open
to the sense of "mystery"

Letter to Women, Message of His Holiness
POPE JOHN PAUL II, July 10

Thank you, women who work
because you take on the responsibilities of men
while still having to be mothers, wives
good little daughters and feminine creatures

Thank you, women who work
because you are the ones we can blame
when the family falls apart

Thank you, women who work
because you make a point to do more
than your fair share
without being paid fairly
even though
no man would do the same for you

Thank you, women who work
for you know you have to prove yourselves
over and over and over again
and that it still isn't enough, so
keep up the good work,

ladies

Ďakujem vám, ženy, ktoré pracujete

Ďakujem vám, ženy, ktoré pracujete
Týmto spôsobom robíte
nenahraditeľný prínos
k rastu kultúry
ktorý spája rozum a cit,
k modelu života stále otvorenému
ku zmyslu "záhady"

List ženám, Posolstvo Jeho Svätosti
PÁPEŽA JÁNA PAVLA II, 10. júla

Ďakujem vám, ženy, ktoré pracujete
pretože preberáte na seba zodpovednosti mužov
zatiaľ čo stále musíte byť matkami, manželkami
dobrými dcéruškami a ženskými stvoreniami

Ďakujem vám, ženy, ktoré pracujete
lebo vy ste tie ktoré môžeme viniť
keď sa rodina rozpadne

Ďakujem Vám, ženy, ktoré pracujete
lebo, si zaumienite urobiť viac
ako je Váš spravodlivý podiel
bez toho aby Vám to bolo zaplatené spravodlivo
aj keď žiadny muž by neurobil to isté pre Vás

Ďakujem Vám, ženy, ktoré pracujete
Lebo viete že si musíte dokázať sami sebe
znova a znova a znova dookola
a že to stále nie je dosť, tak
pokračujte v dobrej práci,

dámy

photograph, Nineteenth Century

that woman   that picture
the images of beauty and softness
of something that shouldn't be touched
that couldn't work   that can't work
the sepia toning oh how ancient
oh the dependency   oh the degradation

my mind has been cluttered
society's a bastard
I can't see the women
I see the hat   the feather
the adornments of beauty
the preposterous impractical way
she has been made to be seen
and not heard

she's only an image
she was forced with an image
is it a shame   is it a sin
and now I've been tainted
with the knowledge of society
with the knowledge of it's motives
and now I can't even see the beauty
I can only see the oppression

"oh, it's not like that anymore" they say
as I wipe the make-up off my eyelids
and wonder who I'm trying to impress

fotografia, devätnáste storočie

tá žena, ten obrázok
obrazy krásy a jemnosti
niečoho, čo malo byť nedotknuté
to nemohlo fungovať, to nemôže fungovať
ach, aký starý   odtieň sépie
ach závislosť ach poníženie

moja myseľ bola preplnená
spoločnosť je bastard
Nevidím ženy
Vidím, klobúk, pierko
ozdoby krásy
groteskne nepraktický spôsob,
bola urobená, aby bola videnou
a nie počutou

ona je len obrázkom
bola jej vnútená predstava
že je to hanba,   hriech
a teraz som bola poškvrnená
znalosťami spoločnosti
znalosťami, ich motívov
a teraz už aj tak nevidím krásu
Vidím len útlak

„Ach, už to tak dávno nie je" hovoria
ako si zotieram make-up z očných viečok
a premýšľam, na koho sa snažím urobiť dojem.html.

Diane Talking About her Trip to Mexico City

So I decided to take a trip to Mexico City.
I decided that this was going to be the
trip I take by myself, this is going to be the
trip where I reclaim my independence.
This is going to be the trip where I venture
out, take on the world, all without help
from a travel companion, from a man.

So I went there, and really, it wasn't as
frightening as I thought it would be.
I needed to learn more of the language,
but otherwise I got along just fine. Oh,
I got lost once, and men in cars kept
offering to give me rides, "hey, baby, you
want your own private taxi?" and I'd have
to move away from them, but one guy
told me which bus I wanted, so I was fine.

But the man that ran the hotel thought it
wasn't safe for me, and he asked me
if my parents loved me, if my family
loved me, if anyone loved me, anyone
at all, because if anyone did, why would
they let me go on this trip alone?

And then as I was touring, I went to an old
church where the was a saint, and they're
considered a saint because their body
doesn't decompose. It's not like religion
in America, because they had to put this
saint's body in a glass case because all
the people who came to see him would
pick off part of his face as a souvenir.

And then as I was touring, I went to a
nunnery, a place where supposedly all the
bad young girls were sent to to live out
the remainder of their days. And
they showed me around in the tour,
and they said, "Here are the crosses that
the young women had to carry when
they walked around in circles in the
courtyard. And these, over here, these
are the crowns of thorns the women
wore." And I looked at the crosses, the
crowns, and there was still blood on them.

This is how things were, I guess. And they
looked at me as strange because I was
taking a trip alone. No one in Mexico City
understood why I'd want to do this there.
No one understood why I'd want to be alone.

Diane hablando sobre su viaje a la Ciudad de México

Entonces decidí hacer un viaje a la Ciudad de México.
Decidí que este iba a ser el
viaje que hago solo, este va a ser el
viaje donde reclamo mi independencia.
Este va a ser el viaje donde me aventuro
fuera, conquistar el mundo, todo sin ayuda
de un compañero de viaje, de un hombre.

Así que fui allí y, en realidad, no fue tan
aterrador como pensé que sería.
Necesitaba aprender más del idioma
pero por lo demás me llevé bien. Oh,
Me perdí una vez, y los hombres en autos se quedaron
ofreciéndome a darme paseos, "oye, buena, tú
¿Quieres tu propio taxi privado?" y yo tendría
alejarme de ellos, pero un chico
me dijo qué autobús quería, así que estaba bien.

Pero el hombre que dirigía el hotel lo pensó
no era seguro para mí, y me preguntó
si mis padres me quisieran, si mi familia
me amaba, si alguien me amaba, alguien
en absoluto, porque si alguien lo hiciera, ¿por qué
me dejaron ir solo en este viaje?

Y luego, mientras estaba de gira, fui a un viejo
iglesia donde era un santo, y es
considerado un santo porque su cuerpo
no se descompone. No es como la religión
en América, porque tenían que poner esto
cuerpo de santo en una vitrina porque todos
la gente que vino a verlo lo haría
quitarle parte de la cara como recuerdo.

Y luego, mientras estaba de gira, fui a un
convento, un lugar donde supuestamente todos
las chicas malas fueron enviadas a vivir
el resto de sus días. Y
me mostraron los alrededores en la gira,
y dijeron: "Aquí están las cruces que
las mujeres jóvenes tuvieron que cargar cuando
Caminaron en círculos en el
patio. Y estos, por aqui, estos
son las coronas de espinas las mujeres
vistió." Y miré las cruces, la
coronas, y todavía tenían sangre.

Así eran las cosas, supongo. Y ellos
me miró como extraño porque estaba
haciendo un viaje solo. Nadie en la Ciudad de Mexico
entendido por qué querría hacer esto allí.
Nadie entendió por qué querría estar solo

A Man Calls a Woman

every time a man calls a woman a "babe"
he tells her he thinks of her as a child
every time a man calls a woman a "fox"
he tells her she is to be treated like an animal
every time a man calls a woman a "honey"
he tells her she is meant to be consumed
every time a man calls a woman a "doll"
he tells her she is something to be played with
every time a man calls a woman a "bag"
he tells her she is something to be used
every time a man calls a woman a "slit"
he tells her she's a body part, not whole
every time a man calls a woman a "screw"
he tells her she is what he does to her
every time a man calls a woman a "girl"
he tells her she can't think like an adult
every time a man calls a woman a "whore"
he tells her she is wrong for having sex
every time a man calls a woman a "lay"
he tells her she is no good on her feet
every time a man calls a woman anything
less than woman he tells her who's the boss
so yes, we all know who the boss is, boys
you've done such a good job of telling us

یک مرد به یک زن اشاره دارد

هر بار که مردی از زن به عنوان "بچه" یاد می کند
او به او می گوید که او را به عنوان یک کودک فکر می کند
هر بار که مردی از زن به عنوان "روباه" یاد می کند
او به او می گوید که باید با او مانند یک حیوان رفتار شود
هر بار که مرد از زن به عنوان "عسل" یاد می کند
او به او می گوید که او قرار است مصرف شود
هر بار که مردی از زن به عنوان "عروسک" یاد می کند
او به او می گوید که او چیزی است که باید با آن بازی کرد
هر بار که مرد از زن به عنوان "کیف" یاد می کند
او به او می گوید که او چیزی برای استفاده است
هر بار که مرد از زن به عنوان "شکاف" یاد می کند
او به او می گوید که او یک عضو بدن است، نه کل
هر بار که مرد از زن به عنوان "پیچ" یاد می کند
او به او می گوید که او همان کاری است که با او انجام می دهد
هر بار که مرد از زن به عنوان "دختر" یاد می کند
او به او می گوید که نمی تواند مانند یک بزرگسال فکر کند
هر بار که مرد از زن به عنوان "فاحشه" یاد می کند
او به او می گوید که برای رابطه جنسی اشتباه می کند
هر بار که مردی از زن به عنوان "لحیم" یاد می کند
او به او می گوید که او روی پاهایش خوب نیست
هر بار که یک مرد به یک زن اشاره می کند
کمتر از زنی که به او می گوید رئیس کیست
پس بله، همه ما می دانیم که رئیس کیست، پسران
خیلی کار خوبی کردی که به ما گفت

In their Homes or In the Streets

you'll never understand

have you ever felt
that everything you did
from the clothes you chose to wear
to the way you styled your hair
to the way you walked down the street
to the way you sat at your desk

to whether you looked at people
as they passed you in the grocery store
when you picked up the food for the family

have you ever felt
that everything you did
was under the scrutiny
of half the world

that a stare could haunt you
if you looked too confident
or your eyes wandered for too long
and actually caught someone's gaze

or your skirt was too short
or you didn't cross your legs

or if you ate a banana
or happened to lick your lips

have you felt it
well, you're not a woman

در خانه هایشان یا در خیابان ها

هرگز نخواهی فهمید

آیا تا به حال احساس کرده اید
که هر کاری کردی
از لباس هایی که برای پوشیدن انتخاب کردی
به روشی که موهایت را حالت دادی
به راهی که در خیابان راه می رفتی
به روشی که پشت میزت نشستی

به اینکه آیا به مردم نگاه کردی
همانطور که در خواربارفروشی از کنار شما گذشتند
وقتی غذای خانواده را برداشتی

آیا تا به حال احساس کرده اید
که هر کاری کردی
تحت نظر بود
از نیمی از جهان

که یک نگاه خیره می تواند شما را آزار دهد
اگر خیلی مطمئن به نظر می رسید
یا چشمان شما برای مدت طولانی سرگردان بود
و در واقع نگاه کسی را جلب کرد

یا دامنت خیلی کوتاه بود
یا پاهایت را روی هم نگذاشتی

یا اگر موز خوردی
یا اتفاقاً لب های شما را لیسید

آیا آن را حس کرده ای
خوب تو زن نیستی

Middle-Class Husbands and Fathers

rapists are not all convicted prisoners
rapists are not all psychopaths
rapists are not all welfare recipients
rapists are not all foaming at the mouth
rapists are not all abused by their parents
rapists are not all sex-depraved
rapists are not all gun-toting criminals
rapists are not all undereducated
rapists are not all jobless
rapists are not all beaten as children
rapists are not all minorities
rapists are not all criminally insane

rapists are in your office
rapists are in your convenience mart
rapists are in your local tavern
rapists are in your school
rapists are in your restaurant
rapists are in your carpool
rapists are in your grocery store
rapists are in your country club
rapists are in your church
rapists are in your family reunion
rapists are in your living room
rapists are in your bedroom

they come in all shapes and sizes
they're everywhere

شوهران و پدران طبقه متوسط

متجاوزان همه زندانیان محکوم نیستند
متجاوزان همه روانی نیستند
متجاوزان همه دریافت کنندگان رفاه نیستند
متجاوزان همگی از دهانشان کف نمی کنند
همه متجاوزان توسط والدین خود مورد آزار و اذیت قرار نمی گیرند
متجاوزان همه از نظر جنسی خوار نیستند
متجاوزان همه جنایتکاران تفنگدار نیستند
متجاوزان همه کم سواد نیستند
متجاوزان همه بیکار نیستند
متجاوزان همه در کودکی مورد ضرب و شتم قرار نمی گیرند
متجاوزان همه اقلیت نیستند
متجاوزان همه از نظر جنایی مجنون نیستند

متجاوزین در دفتر شما هستند
متجاوزان به راحتی در خدمت شما هستند
متجاوزین در میخانه محلی شما هستند
متجاوزین در مدرسه شما هستند
متجاوزین در رستوران شما هستند
متجاوزین در کارپول شما هستند
متجاوزین در خواربار فروشی شما هستند
متجاوزین در کلوپ کشور شما هستند
متجاوزین در کلیسای شما هستند
متجاوزان در جمع خانواده شما هستند
متجاوزین در اتاق نشیمن شما هستند
متجاوزین در اتاق خواب شما هستند

آنها در همه اشکال و اندازه ها هستند
آنها همه جا هستند

Most Accurate Metaphors

now there's two ways
this can happen, little girl
you can keep fighting me,
and if that's the case, I'll
have to keep my hand
over your mouth and
this knife at your neck,
or you can relax, enjoy
yourself, make this easier
on the both of us

you know you want this
so stop fighting it

I saw the way you were
looking at me earlier,
the way you stared at me
the way you were dressed
I know what you were thinking
so don't say a word

did you think those drinks
were free

how long did you think
I could wait
It's my turn now
you owe it to me

just do as I say
and no one gets hurt

دقیق ترین استعاره ها

حالا دو راه هست
این ممکن است اتفاق بیفتد، دختر کوچک
تو میتونی به جنگ من ادامه بدی
و اگر اینطور باشد، خواهم کرد
باید دستم را نگه دارد
بالای دهانت و
،این چاقو در گردن شما
یا می توانید استراحت کنید، لذت ببرید
خودت این کار رو راحت تر کن
روی هر دوی ما

میدونید که این رو میخواید
پس از مبارزه با آن دست بردارید

من اینطوری که تو بودی دیدم
،زودتر به من نگاه کرد
جوری که به من خیره شدی
طرز لباس پوشیدنت
میدونم به چی فکر میکردی
پس یک کلمه حرف نزن

فکر کردی اون نوشیدنی ها
رایگان بودند

چقدر فکر کردی
میتونستم صبر کنم
الان نوبت منه
تو مدیون من هستی

فقط به قول من عمل کن
و هیچ کس صدمه نمی بیند

the Measuring Scale

Why don't you dissect me,
take every single part of me
and equate it with power tools,
sports and violence?
Bang me, screw me, nail me,
hammer me, bag me, pump
me. Shoot it in me. Maybe you
can even score.

If we're talking about
measuring scales, what about
the scale that defines the way
you treat us:
on one end is the minor stuff,
calling us 'baby' and 'sugar,'
whistling as we walk by, but
then move along the scale, get to
the blonde jokes, yes, they're so
funny, then how about a pinch
in the rear at the office,
well, that's harmless enough
and while you're at it, porn
movies and magazines, what harm
do they do, and hey, women
have always worked at home,
so you should have all the jobs
and get the better pay anyway
and since we're just your pro-
perty, fuck us whenever you
want, I mean, hey, you're doing
it already in every other aspect
of our repressed, oppressed lives
so rape us, smack us around
knock us down a flight of stairs
that's what we're here for

god, I don't even know how to
measure these things anymore

مقیاس اندازه گیری

،چرا من را تشریح نمی کنی
تک تک اجزای وجودم را بگیر
،و آن را با ابزارهای برقی برابر بدانیم
ورزش و خشونت؟
،بکوبم، بکوبم، بکوبم
مرا چکش کن، کیفم کن، پمپاژ کن
من به من شلیک کن شاید تو
.حتی می تواند گلزنی کند

اگر صحبت می کنیم
مقیاس های اندازه گیری، چه در مورد
مقیاسی که راه را مشخص می کند
:شما با ما رفتار می کنید
،در یک طرف چیزهای جزئی است
،ما را "عزیزم "و "شکر "صدا می کنند
وقتی از کنار ما رد می‌شویم سوت می‌کشیم، اما
سپس در امتداد مقیاس حرکت کنید، به آن برسید
بلوند شوخی می کند، بله، آنها چنین هستند
خنده دار است، پس چگونه در مورد یک خرج کردن
،در قسمت عقب در دفتر
خوب، به اندازه کافی بی ضرر است
و در حالی که در آن هستید، پورن
فیلم ها و مجلات، چه مضراتی
آیا آنها انجام می دهند، و هی، زنان
،همیشه در خانه کار کرده اند
بنابراین شما باید همه مشاغل را داشته باشید
و به هر حال دستمزد بهتری دریافت کنید
و از آنجایی که ما فقط طرفدار شما هستیم
پرتی، هر وقت که داری لعنت به ما
می خواهی، یعنی هی، داری انجام می دهی
آن را در حال حاضر در هر جنبه دیگر
از زندگی سرکوب شده و سرکوب شده ما
پس به ما تجاوز کن، ما را بکوب
یک پله ما را به زمین بزن
برای همین اینجا هستیم

خدایا من حتی بلد نیستم
این چیزها را دیگر اندازه بگ

the Men at the Construction Site

a woman told me
that scientists did an experiment
where a woman
first walked past a construction site
with her head down

no one bothered her,
no one noticed her
everyone at the site left her alone

then, later in the day,
she walked past again
in the same outfit, with the same stride
but this time she walked with
her head up,
more confidently

and that's when she got
the calls, the whistles
from the men at the construction site

and you tell me it's not deliberate
and you tell me it's not an effort
to keep women in their place

مردان در محل ساخت و ساز

زنی به من گفت
که دانشمندان آزمایشی انجام دادند
جایی که یک زن
ابتدا از کنار یک محل ساخت و ساز گذشت
با سرش پایین

کسی اذیتش نکرد
هیچ کس متوجه او نشد
همه در سایت او را تنها گذاشتند

سپس، در اواخر روز،
دوباره از کنارش گذشت
با همان لباس، با همان گام
اما این بار او با آن راه رفت
سرش را بالا،
با اطمینان بیشتر

و این زمانی بود که او گرفت
تماس ها، سوت ها
از مردان در محل ساخت و ساز

و تو به من می گویی که عمدی نیست
و شما به من می گویید که این یک تلاش نیست
برای نگه داشتن زنان در جای خو

Content with Inferior Men

There are some theorists that say
that women need to be able to look up to a man
in order to feel complete. These theorists
would say that a woman could not be president,
at least not on a personal level.
Think of it - here is a woman, the most important
person on earth, and she would never know of anyone
who had more power than her. How could she
look up to any man? How could she admire
any man? How could she respect any man?
And you know, I can kind of see that point,
how can you love someone you don't respect,
I mean, I want someone in my life that can teach
me something, that can help me grow, and if
I was the most powerful person on earth
I would probably think that no one could teach
me anything. But the only thing I could think of
in response to this theory is, why don't men
who are the presidents of the United States
of America find themselves unhappy with their
boring, unequal, supportive wives? Why is it
that men are content with inferior women
but women aren't content with inferior men?

اما زنان به مردان پست راضی

برخی از نظریه پردازان هستند که می گویند
که زنان باید بتوانند به یک مرد نگاه کنند
به منظور احساس کامل بودن این نظریه پردازان
می گویند که یک زن نمی تواند رئیس جمهور شود،
حداقل نه در سطح شخصی
به آن فکر کنید ـ اینجا یک زن است، مهمترین چیز
کسی روی زمین است و او هرگز کسی را نمی شناسد
که از او قدرت بیشتری داشت چگونه او می تواند
به هر مردی نگاه کن؟ چگونه می توانست تحسین کند
هر مردی؟ چگونه می تواند به هر مردی احترام بگذارد؟
و می دانید، من می توانم آن نقطه را به نوعی ببینم،
چگونه می توانید کسی را دوست داشته باشید که به او احترام نمی گذارید،
یعنی من کسی را در زندگی ام می خواهم که بتواند آموزش دهد
من چیزی، که می تواند به من کمک کند رشد کنم، و اگر
من قدرتمندترین فرد روی زمین بودم
من احتمالا فکر می کنم که هیچ کس نمی تواند تدریس کند
من از هر چیزی اما تنها چیزی که می توانستم به آن فکر کنم
در پاسخ به این نظریه این است که چرا مردان این کار را نمی کنند
که رؤسای جمهور ایالات متحده هستند
آمریکا خود را از آنها ناراضی می بینند
همسران خسته کننده، نابرابر و حامی؟ چرا
که مردان به زنان پست قانع می شوند
اما زنان به مردان پست راضی نیستند؟

I'm Thinking About Myself Too Much

all of my life it
has all been about you
what do you need
what do you want
how can I help you
what can I do for you
and now for once
I start to live
and now you tell me
that I'm thinking about
myself too much
and I think back to
all the time I've
spent with you
and all the care
I've given you
and now you tell me
that I'm thinking about
myself too much
and I've cooked for
you and I've cleaned
for you and I've made
sure everything in
your world made sense
and now you tell me
that I'm thinking about
myself too much
and all I can think
is that you're only angry
because I'm thinking
about me at all

من بیش از حد به خودم فکر می کنم

تمام زندگی من آن را
همه چیز درباره شما بوده است
چه چیزی نیاز دارید
چه چیزی می خواهید
چگونه می توانم به شما کمک کنم
چه کاری می توانم برای شما انجام دهم
و حالا برای یک بار
شروع میکنم به زندگی کردن
و حالا تو به من بگو
که دارم بهش فکر میکنم
خودم خیلی زیاد
و من به عقب فکر می کنم
تمام زمانی که من دارم
با شما سپری کرد
keh و تمام مراقبت
من به شما داده ام
و حالا تو به من بگو
که دارم بهش فکر میکنم
خودم خیلی زیاد
و من آشپزی کرده ام
من و تو تمیز کردیم
برای تو و من ساخته ام
مطمئن باشید همه چیز در
دنیای شما معنا پیدا کرد
و حالا تو به من بگو
که دارم بهش فکر میکنم
خودم خیلی زیاد
و تمام چیزی که می توانم فکر کنم
این است که شما فقط عصبانی هستید
چون دارم فکر میکنم
اصلا در مورد من

Against My Will

There have been so many times
When I was raped

When a man
Held me down
Forced himself on me
Against my will

That way is just too obvious

And the "someone tried
to beat me up"?
That is old news

If you have done this research
If you have gone through this
If you have lived this life...

But I should be above this
I should be a Feminist
With a capital F

I guess with that in mind
I should not mind the cat calls
Or the whistles

Or the fact that the word "woman"
Is the word "man"
With a couple of letters tacked on

Like how "she" is "he" with an "s"

Like we're an extension of them

Or the fact that men
First look at me
By looking at my breasts
And not my eyes

I should be aware
That a woman with power
Instills fear
And a woman with power in a company
Can still be demoted outside of the company
Where she can still be ridiculed

I can handle the jokes
About being a blond
Or being dumb
Or being both

I can hear the line
they say insultingly
That we HAVE to be irrational
Because we are so damn emotional

I mean
How do you trust someone
who bleeds for five days every month
And won't die?

Fine
If they want to degrade
Everything that makes us strong
Fine
If they say we can not hold a job
Fine
We will just depend on you for money
And also work our jobs
On our time
And keep money for OUR little nest-egg

And how much money
are you boys going to have
when it comes to the end of your family line?
How much of a life
are you boys going to have
when it comes to the end of your family line?
How much happiness?

Prieš Mano valią

Buvo tiek kartų
Kai buvau išprievartauta

Kai vyras
Laikė mane žemyn
Prisivertė mane
Prieš mano valią

Toks būdas per daug akivaizdus

Ir „kažkas bandė
kad mane sumuštų"?
Tai sena naujiena

Jei atlikote šį tyrimą
Jei išgyvenote tai
Jei gyvenote šį gyvenimą...

Bet aš turėčiau būti aukščiau už tai
Aš turėčiau būti feministė
Su didžiąja raide F

Manau, turėdamas tai omenyje
Neturėčiau prieštarauti katės skambučiams
Arba švilpukai

Arba tai, kad žodis „moteris"
Ar žodis "vyras"
Su pora raidžių priklijuotų

Kaip „ji" yra „jis" su raide „s"

Lyg mes būtume jų pratęsimas

Arba tai, kad vyrai
Pirmiausia pažvelk į mane
Žiūrėdamas į mano krūtis
Ir ne mano akys

turėčiau žinoti
Kad moteris su galia
Sukelia baimę
Ir moteris, turinti valdžią įmonėje
Vis dar gali būti pažemintas už įmonės ribų
Kur iš jos dar galima tyčiotis

Galiu susitvarkyti su juokeliais
Apie buvimą blondine
Arba kvailas
Arba būti abiem

Aš girdžiu eilutę
jie sako įžeidžiamai
Kad mes TURIME būti neracionalūs
Nes mes tokie velniškai emocingi

turiu omeny
Kaip kažkuo pasitiki
kuris kas mėnesį kraujuoja penkias dienas
Ir nemirs?

gerai
Jei jie nori degraduoti
Viskas, kas daro mus stiprius
gerai
Jei jie sako, kad negalime dirbti
gerai
Mes tiesiog priklausysime nuo jūsų pinigų
Taip pat dirbame savo darbus
Mūsų laiku
Ir pasilik pinigų MŪSŲ mažam lizdeliui-kiaušiniui

Ir kiek pinigų
ar jūs, vaikinai, turėsite
kai kalba eina apie tavo šeimos linijos pabaigą?
Kiek daug gyvenimo
ar jūs, vaikinai, turėsite
kai kalba eina apie tavo šeimos linijos pabaigą?
Kiek laimės?

Oriental

Years ago
Chinese women
bound their feet with cloths
forcing them to remain
the foot of a child

The smaller the foot
the higher the class
the more helpless the woman
the more she needed a husband
to care for her

It was normal
for the daughter to cry
and cry
at the thought
of hurting her feet so
of being unable to walk

Of crippling herself

But the mother knew better

The girl would never find
a suitable husband
if her feet
were like those
of a servant

At least
a working servant

handcuffs
are like swatches of cheesecloth
slowing wrapping
layer upon layer
upon layer

The tears falling
land
in her lap

a pattern
as the daughter sobs
and rocks back and forth

东方的

几年前

中国妇女

用布包住他们的脚
迫使他们留下
孩子的脚

脚越小
等级越高
女人越无助
她越需要丈夫
照顾她

这很正常

..让女儿哭
哭泣
一想到
伤了她的脚
无法行走

残废自己

但妈妈更清楚

女孩永远找不到
合适的丈夫
如果她的脚
就像那些
仆人的

至少
..一个工作的仆人

手铐
就像一块块粗棉布
减慢包装
层层
一层一层

眼泪落下大地
在她的腿上

一种模式
当女儿抽泣时
来回晃动

Modern Day Footbindings and
the Oppression of Women

I have never been one to think about my predicament. It's a common predicament-- I have to face it every day of my life, and it indirectly causes me problems wherever I go. I can't walk alone at night because of it. I can't look a male stranger straight in the eye because of it. I have to worry about the kind of clothes I wear, the implications of the statements I make, and even the way I walk because of it. But I've never given it a second thought.

My predicament is that I am a woman. At first it doesn't seem to sound like a predicament at all, but the more one thinks about the lack of freedom sentenced to a woman solely because she is a woman, the word 'predicament' becomes more of an understatement. In this male-oriented society, women are reduced to objects: pornography sells more than the top news magazines, the videos that MTV broadcast flaunt the woman's body for just anyone to see, and instances of rape are at an all-time high. Women today are held down by forces that are blind to many - society has evidently become a jail cell so large that its prisoners cannot even see the bars. But there are bars, and if we only look for them and see them for what they really are, we may then be able to make the changes that will make this society a more equal one. And a safer one.

In China, one man created the custom of wrapping up the woman's foot so tightly that it restricted the woman's walking because it caused so much pain. It was a way for men to be sure that women in their society were entirely dependent on them. In many third world countries, women are forced to wear dresses that cover up their entire body, for one man has no right to look at another man's possessions. They call it tradition. If this is so, then tradition dehumanizes the woman.

Even in the United States these bindings are all around us, and these indirect restrictions are so commonplace that we have failed to notice that they are even there, keeping us "in our place". I will only give one example. I feel that only one example is necessary.

I used to get a subscription to a women's magazine. I enjoyed flipping through the pages of Glamour, even if it did only make me feel inadequate as a woman and as a person. As I read, as I flipped through the pages and saw the photographs of beautiful women staring me in the face telling me that I was no good unless I was beautiful and was able to attract the best looking men, I began to feel that I had to change my image in order to become the objectified model that society had typecast to be "the best". These women's magazines devote about one fourth of their contents to careers, and probably about three fourths of their magazines to looking good. These magazines focused on looking like the stereotypical woman, looking sexy, and doing this all for a man. That's half of the problem right there.

But just the other day I looked through a neighbor's recent issue of Glamour magazine, and I came to a startling realization. As I flipped through the colossal number of advertisements that appear in the first half of these magazines (you often can't find an article until you reach page 50), I looked at the women. I looked at the underlying messages that these advertisements were relaying. And I couldn't believe my eyes.

Here is an example that illustrates my point. "Every Valentine Needs A Hero." The quote itself, from one of the first ads that I saw, gives the impression that a woman needs a man in order to survive. As romantic as the ad may look, I couldn't help but notice the subtle signs: the woman is lying down on the bed, looking up at the man; the man is standing over her, looking down on her. Her back is turned to the camera, so that you can't see the expressions on her face and so that you can't see her humanness. The woman's arms are crossed, evidently covering herself. A rose is placed right in the middle of the tray (remember-- nothing in advertising isn't planned). Yes, the man is the hero, and the woman needs him for support. How would she function otherwise?

"Valentine... I got you just what you wanted." This ad, as I looked at the couple plastered on the page, seemed to scream "submission" to me. As the woman's face is turned toward the man, she is turned away from the camera - and becomes more of a body than an actual woman. Her arms are folded around him in a way that makes the viewer feel that she is clinging on to the only thing that matters to her. Furthermore, the two wide silver bracelets on her hands give the impression that she is handcuffed-- attached to the man, whether or not by force. The man, however, is merely smiling (maybe "smirking" is a better word) as he looks away from the woman. His happiness seems to stem from the fact that he has this relatively valuable possession.

Even the words in this advertisement are misleading. How handy it is that the woman has given her man just what he wanted. And she should, too. It's her duty. She's a woman. And what exactly did she get him? Why, "she got him a year of..." wait a minute, let's put a little pause in there, one just long enough to make your mind wander... "GQ". This relatively innocent ad has taken on a different meaning altogether in this new light.

Then I turned the page and saw another advertisement--and it appeared to be a centerfold. My only question was: how on earth is a clothing company supposed to advertise clothes when the clothes are barely on the model? Then, I'm afraid to say, I answered my own question. This company, like most others, isn't advertising for the product that they are selling, for their products have become the means to another end, as opposed to the end itself. They are advertising an image-- an image of the woman being dependent on her looks in order to achieve success. Keep in mind that this - good looks - is the possible extent of a woman's success. The concept of talent has seemed to fall by the wayside.

After looking at the images that bombarded me, I couldn't help but wonder if I was reacting rather harshly. But then I began to think: what about the images that you see on billboards? What about the flaunting of women on television programs and commercials? What are these images teaching the children of today - the adults of tomorrow that will shape society?   I couldn't help but wonder if these signals were related to the increase in crimes against woman that are so prevalent today. If they are related, when will this ever change?   Or will we be forever bound to the system?

Needless to say, I don't get those magazines anymore. I try to explain to others how women are metaphorically abused between the glossy pages of these magazines. But it's only one source. One of many. And it seems that even if we as women were capable of removing one form of this degradation, other bars would still be up to keep us in our cell. Only until we break down the walls will we be able to say that we are free.

a book for men

It occurred to me when I decided to do this project in 1991 that there were so many more derogatory terms for women than there were for men. Then I started to think about the actual names themselves and I noticed a few themes:

1. Many terms, both terms considered "nice" and terms considered "rude," were less-than-human, whether they be inanimate objects, animals, foods, or what have you, that somehow became descriptions for women.

2. There was a much greater number of "mean" slang terms for women who were promiscuous than for men (for men, it was something to be proud of, so slang terms were not derogatory but complimentary).

3. There was a much greater incidence of jokes and phrases about women being either stupid or promiscuous than men.

4. Terms for sex with women (terms used predominantly by men) were often sports analogies, references to power tools and other historically masculine objects, or by nature violent.

I originally thought of taking photographs of what these terms really are (and not of their slang definition) in order to show how ludicrous the contrast was to what the terms have come to mean in our society.

The jump to make the following pages a reference tool for men in order to help them degrade women with their terminology was to provide an additional point of contrast: these pages, the way they are designed, are to make it look like this name-calling is a conscious effort on the part of all men to degrade women with the terms they use.

The reason why I did this is because although the effort is not made consciously, and although this conscious effort as displayed on the following pages seems humorous, the current effect of this spectrum of terms for women has the same result as if it was a concerted movement. No, it isn't a concerted movement: it's worse; it is second nature to everyone. After realizing this, I felt that displaying these points humorously and sarcastically would make it a better engine for making people think about the language they use in describing women.

Hey, all you **men** out there - do you

remember the time when **life was simple** –

when a **man** was a **man**

and a wo**man** knew her place?

Well, we think it's time **you had your say.**
Introducing the man's guide

for **derogatory**

terms for wo**men!!**

Be **vicious!** Be **malicious!**

Put wo**men in their place!**

Now, the key to degrading women is to **call them names**

that are **less than human.**

You can easily do this by calling wo**men**

anything from **animals** to **plant life**

to **food** to **inanimate objects.**
(We know they're thinking adults, but by

calling them names that are less than that, they will

eventually feel like **less than human beings.)**

To start off, you can call wo**men** names that are less than adults

(By referring to them as **children,** like **baby, babe** or

girl. terms like these are less effective, since they are so commonplace,

but can still **degrade** wo**men,** so use them liberally…)

These terms can even sound like **compliments**

so **they won't complain!**

Try terms like **baby** or **babe**, for example

or call someone a **girl**…

Or how about degrading women by calling them animals

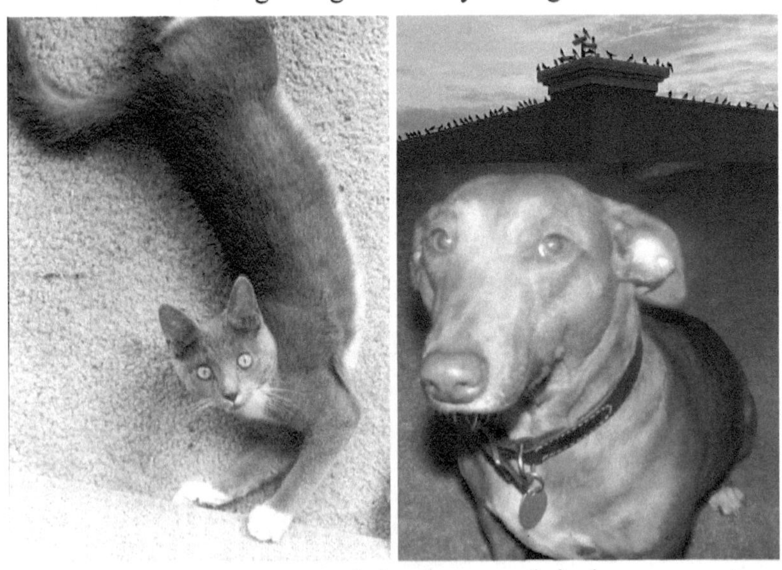

Use **pussy**, or **bitch**, or **chick**—
or refer to their **body parts**,
like their **hooters** or her **beaver**!

How about degrading woMen by calling them kinds of food, like a piece of meat, or refer to her body parts as food,

like melons — or call them a honey or a pumpkin…

These are good ones, because it has become an affectionate term, but still refers to woMen as non-thinking items for human consumption!

Can you think of any others? She's a **peach!**
What about her **cherry?** Or call her **sugar**, or **tomato?**

You can try **sweet pea, cheesecake, cupcake or muffin!**

Don't forget her private parts are

Tang!?! If you call her a **dish** it sounds like
she's to be **consumed** instead of **treated with respect!**

But degrading women by calling them kinds of animals
or kinds of food only begins to scratch the surface…
There are other ways to turn women into objects…
you can refer to their body parts
instead of them as a whole human being or you can even
objectify the act of sex!

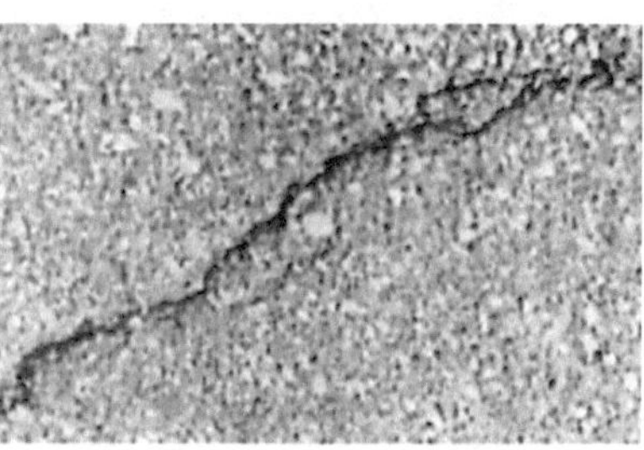

Degrade women by defining them by their body parts!
Call them a hoe, refer to their crack, or their bush,

Or even their hole too!

Because if you can't define women by their body parts, what good are they? But wait, there's more, don't forget her **box**!

Or refer to her **knockers**...

Her **jugs,** her rack or her **slit!**

Degrade women by calling them inanimate objects, like a **doll!**

Put your mind to it, the derogatory terms for wo**men** are endless!

How about **degrading** wo**men** by making sex with them **violent**, like to **bag** or to **bang!**

Bagging and **Banging** work…

If they get **out of line**, try **bopping!**

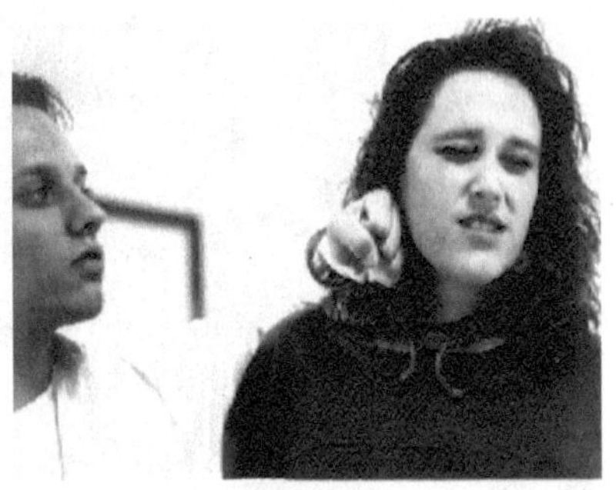

When it comes to having sex with wo**men**, **construction terminology** and **sports analogies** work well too!

Hammering, pumping, scoring, screwing—

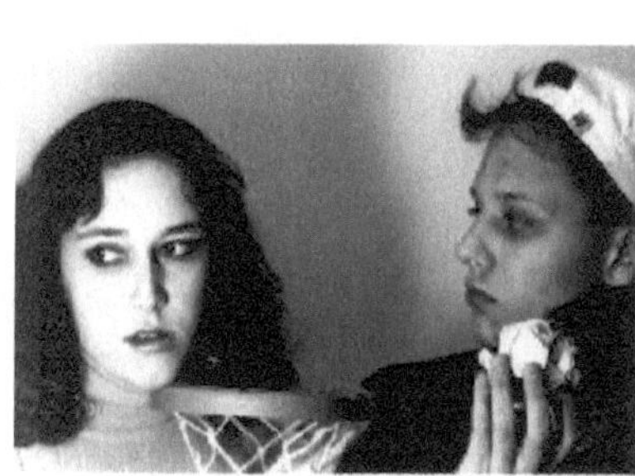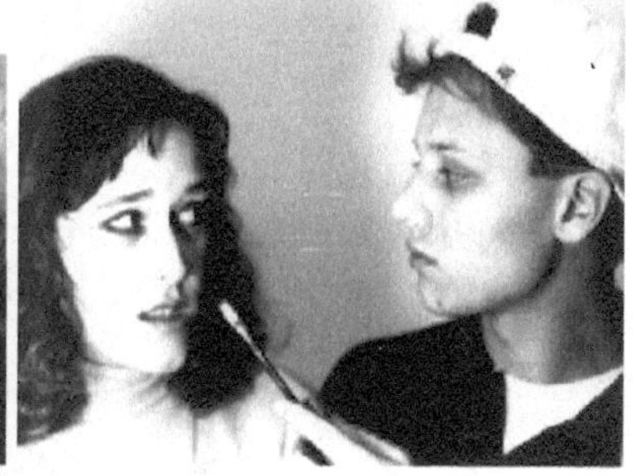

and don't forget **nailing** her too!!!

Separate the wo**men** from the sex with **sports,** **power tools** and **violence**

and then the wo**men** won't matter at all!

Try some **degrading jokes** about wo**men!**

what do wo**men** and beer bottles
have in common?

they're both **empty** from the neck up!

why do wo**men** wear panties?
to keep their ankles warm!

what's the difference between a wo**man**
and a bowling ball? you can only put
three fingers in a bowling ball!

what do you call a **prostitute** and three
blondes walking down the street?
regular price, 4 bucks, 4 bucks, 4 bucks!

why is a beer better than a wo**man?**
it will always give you a head
and will never **talk back** to you!

what makes a perfect wo**man?**
a flat head, three feet tall and no teeth!

what is the flabby skin around a vagina?
a wo**man!**

Try some degrading phrases
for women!

call then sluts!
she can't wrestle, but you should see her box
call them whores!
call them rags!
liquor in the front, poker in the rear
call them bimbos!
call them cunts!
smells like fish, tastes like chicken
call them skanks!
call them anything that defines them
as a sexual object!

make women feel stupid!
make women inadequate!
make women inferior!
then they will be!

and remember, men - degrading women
isn't just for fun.
it's tradition,
it's the way we stay ahead.
it's our way of life!
So keep up the good work!

# of Independence or Freedom

So it seems you cram us in here
like we're sardines.
How many of us have you crammed in here
before you send us on our way?

Strap us in, make sure
we don't get any strange ideas
of independence or freedom
('cause really, you wouldn't want us

to think for ourselves)...

Strap us in, compartmentalize us —
but the thing is, you thought
I was just like everyone else,
that I'd just sit back and take it.

These sardines around me
seem totally complacent —
what have you told them
to make the so subservient?

Well, maybe you didn't get it before
but I'll take a sledgehammer to your plans.
I'll shatter that glass ceiling
and that two-way mirror

you watch us through.

I don't care where you think
you're taking us,
and I no longer care
if you're sending us away.

I didn't sign up for this ride,
and being crammed in here
is making me nauseous.
Don't make me throw up

before I start my revolt,
because whether or not
you think we're sardines, and want
to cram us away like we're nothing,

just remember:

I'm bigger than my ego lets on
and I'll take whatever makeshift
weapon I can find, to break free
of how you think we should be.

Too Far (2020 edit)

When he met me
he told me
I looked like
Gwyneth Paltrow,
Cameron Diaz,
Kim Basinger —
long blonde locks

but as time
wore on I knew
I wasn't her
and I could never
be her   and I was
never good enough
thin enough
pretty enough

so I got a perm
straightened my
teeth
bought a wonder
bra   but it wasn't
doing the trick

I bought SlimFast
used the stair
stepper   ate rice
cakes and wheat
germ but I wasn't
thin enough   I
only dropped
twenty pounds

so I went to the
spa   got my skin
peeled   soaked
myself in mud
wrapped myself
in cellophane
bought the amino
acid facial creams
but I knew they
didn't really
work

so I went to
the doctor   got my
nose slimmed
my tummy stapled
my thighs sucked

thought about
getting a rib or two
removed
you know
like Cher

but I figured
my ribs?
they've got to
be there for
something
and hey, that's
just going
too far

Kurt Irons (it's just a girl)

Kurt Irons
was arrested
and charged
with vehicular
homicide

Kurt Irons
while intoxicated
stole a truck
and drove it
straight
into another truck
and killed
a thirty-seven-year-old woman

according to police reports,
Kurt Irons
was
surprised
by the arrest
by the fact
that he was charged
with vehicular
homicide

Kurt Irons
was quoted
as saying

"dudes
it's just a
girl,
man

it's a girl -
nothing
but a
girl"

Marilyn Monroe Falling Through the Cracks

some people would have
called me a slut
I prefer a vixen

Personally, I don't think
I was doing anything wrong
I had it all
men adored me

most men would have done
the same thing I did
played the field

I wasn't even looking for sex
just companionship

I changed my name
got rid of the old boring me
'til I was "new and improved"

changed whatever I could about me
'til I couldn't recognize myself any longer

and I had the fame
I had the wealth, the looks
everything

I wore those stiletto heels
I stepped over the cracks
that could have sent me tumbling

why would I want one man
keeping me in place
maybe I'd borrow a man's arm
to help me step over
those cracks on my way,
but what if I wanted to see
a bit more of life
through the eyes of other people —
why am I resented for that?

so I start seeing my ex again
and another ex
and a new guy
and another

you know, most men
would normally love to have
a no-strings attached relationship
with a woman

why couldn't that happen with me
why is it people
become obsessed with me

this person I've created,
this person that isn't me:
is what I've created
really that famous,
that perfect?

I have rejected some men
so many times
they had to pick up their ego
from between he cracks
of the dirty floor,
but they keep coming back
telling me they love me
wanting me to love them back

I know I brought this upon myself
I wanted to go on this wild ride

but I don't know how much facial cream
I can use to keep hiding those cracks
forming around my eyes,
I know I say "keep smiling"
but those deep lines
around this "vivacious smile"
are now cracks in my armor,
growing deeper and deeper
with every milestone I reach

I know I brought this upon myself
I wanted to go on this wild ride
but I didn't want to carry any baggage

I thought I could make the men
carry it for me

and it seems that my bags
are getting heavier
and it seems that the bags
under my eyes
won't go away anymore

those bags are getting heavier,
there are more cracks in the road

and everything now is so heavy

Oh, She Was a Woman

She was a woman who thought too much.
She was a woman who accomplished everything she set out to.
She was a woman who wore a crown of thorns.
She was a woman who was punished for things she had not done.

She was a woman who was strong,
         who was beautiful,
         who was beaten down,
         and she
         got
         angry.

She was a woman who would walk into a coworker's office,
stand on a desk and do the twist,
just to relieve corporate boredom.

She was a woman who worked eighteen-hour days
         because
she was a woman who's brain was always on.
She was a woman who fought for her rights.
And

she was a woman who should not have been born.

She was a woman who wrote poetry.
She was a woman who believed in nothing but herself
         and trust me,
         she
         deserved
         more.

She was a woman who would jump on hotel beds
every time she travelled and booked a room.
Because it was hers. Because she could.

She was a woman who belched out loud,
        she laughed too hard,
        she swore too much.
        And she grew up too fast.

She was a woman who worked on eight different projects
at once, and still managed to get them all done on time.

She was a woman who never lost control.
        She planned everything,
        she demanded perfection, and
        she always had the answers.

She was a woman who raised the pitch of her voice
when she was asking for something.

She was a woman who never played drinking games,
because she never needed an excuse to drink.
        Because she could drink most men under the table.
        She loved dirty jokes, and
        she seldom crossed her legs.

She was a woman who wanted to feel alive.
She was a woman who could not eat something she could not kill.
        She wrote letters to the editor,
        and when that wasn't enough
        she became an editor, because
        she liked making waves.

Because she was a woman who knew all to well
that you only had one life to live.
Don't do something because it's expected of you,
do it because you are a woman who knows what's right.
That golden ring is almost in your grasp.
You've got the brains,
and believe it or not,
you've got the brawn,
so don't let anything stand in your way.

Sexism in General

As I grew up, I did what I thought was expected of me. I didn't bring up unmentionable subjects to my parents. I didn't burp out loud. I didn't complain. And I didn't know why.

And it wasn't that my parents, or my teachers, or my peers, were trying to cram a certain lifestyle down my throat. It was just the norm, what was expected, what everyone was used to.

But the more time I spent on my own, the more I questioned how I was supposed to act, what I was supposed to say, how I was supposed to dress, what I was supposed to like. I saw the way men treated women in relationships, how women primarily reacted to the things that men did instead of acting on their own. I also saw women feel like they were being pushed around, like they were being treated unfairly.

And then I saw some statistics about rape. That one in four women will be raped by the time they leave college; that one in three women will be raped in their lifetime. That over eighty percent of college-age rapes are committed by someone the victim knew.

Then I thought of how women are degraded and objectified in pornography, or how they are treated unfairly in the workplace. There is a different set of rules for women to follow versus men in society, and all of those rules are designed to let women know that their place is behind men.

I looked at history. Wedding ceremonies have had the father give away his daughter — his possession — to a man she could love, honor and obey, in a ceremony conducted by a man under the rule of a male god. Virgin women have even been sacrificed throughout history to assorted gods. Ancient Chinese adolescent women had their feet bound for months so their feet would be petite, but deformed and useless for walking, because the inability to move was considered attractive to rich men. Some tribes have made it a custom to add tight rings around women's necks, continually adding more, to elongate the neck, while other tribes pierce women's ears and put successively larger rings inside the holes, to stretch the ear lobe down past the shoulder. Women were hunted and killed in colonial America for being witches — when they were in fact no more than individuals who practiced independent, rational thought in a society that didn't like their women to think.

I looked at the way our parents were raised. The woman was expected to work only during war time, and then only to assist men or to work in menial tasks. They were otherwise expected to cook for the family, to clean the house, and to please the husband. The man was the owner of his castle, worked during the day to make this life possible for his family, and expected to be pampered by his wife and children when he got home.

Then I looked at the way I was raised. I was given dolls and pretty pink dresses and was encouraged to play with my best friend indoors instead of roughhousing outside with a group. My hair was long, and curled for special occasions. I had to listen to my elders, especially the male ones.

Then I looked around me. Advertising and Hollywood demanded beautiful bodies for their brainless women, who blindly followed their leading man. The workplace had female secretaries serving the male CEOs, wearing skirts and make-up and panty hose and high heels and being called "babe." Speaking of language, even the language I heard around me — from being called a pumpkin to a tomato to a peach — made me feel like I was placed on this earth to be consumed, not to be a human being.

This is when I started to work for acquaintance rape education groups, running seminars, making posters and brochures and the like for women who were in pain and felt like they had no place else to turn. And the more I saw this pain on such a wide scale, the angrier I got. I'm an intelligent woman, I thought, and I as well as all women don't deserve to be treated like this.

Although I am no longer working for any women's groups, I still feel like I am fighting. But what I am fighting for and how I am fighting for it is different from how the average person thinks of a woman "crusader." I am fighting for people to look at women as people first, before they assume that women are less intelligent, less strong, or less valuable. I am fighting, through my writing, through the way I think, through my example, for men to think of women as being on the same level as them, to look at women as their equals. I am fighting for feminism.

The definition of feminism, according to Webster's Ninth New Collegiate Dictionary, is "the theory of the political, economic and social equality of the sexes." That's it. It doesn't mean women should get a job before a man just because she's a woman and has had bad breaks. It doesn't mean women have to dress and look like men if they don't want to. It doesn't mean pornography should be made illegal, and it doesn't mean all women should hate all men.

In practice, it means we should have the same opportunities as men. The choice to take these opportunities is up to the individual — not up to their sex. In theory, it means we should not be looked at as inferiors solely because we are female. In other words, we should not be treated unfairly because of the choices that we as individuals make, if we have every right to make those choices.

It is because of the way that women are looked at in society that there are political economic and social disparities between the sexes. It is because of ideas, not laws. And yes, there have been laws separating genders, and it has taken far too long for those laws to be abolished, but even when laws are lifted, that doesn't mean the ideas the male gender holds about women change because of any law. These ideas create a spectrum of sexism that starts at things as innocent as jokes and cute nicknames, moves to catcalls in the street to harassment in the workplace to unequal pay for equal work, and then moves on to things as cruel and as painful as wife-beating and rape. All of these things, severe or tame, stem from the idea that women are inferior and all of these things contribute to the inequality between the sexes. They all are manifestations of the same idea, only at different degrees.

A friend of mine told me about how in the Soviet Union, after the revolution, Stalin and the government wanted to make sure all people were equal — that women were free from their economic dependence on men — so they enacted laws to make women work and industrialize the country. But ideas about the role of women in society did not change, and in the post-revolution economic crisis, not only then did the women have to work, but they also had to stand in line for rations of bread. Household chores were still women's tasks; the rules changed, but the ideas stayed the same. When women were asked whether they were happier after the revolution or before, they said before, because at least then they didn't have to work as well as do their expected chores.

I'm not trying to enact any laws. I'm not trying to twist anyone's arm. A change doesn't occur in a free society by forcing rules down people's throats.

What I am trying to do is make both men and women think about the conflicts between the sexes in all of their manifestations, why they occur, and what effect they have on our society. To think. And then to act.

Finally Treated Fairly (what we need in life)

After the cards have been stacked against women for millennia
women struggle through this gamble of life
(even though they know full well the house always wins)

but like a chant you can hear around the world,
what we women need in life is what all people need in life —
we need to be treated as equals; we need the respect we deserve

We women can hear the battle cry around the world,
"que necesitamos en la vida" shouted in Español,
"was wir auf das Leben brauchen" proclaimed in Germany,
"Co potrzelujemy w zyciu" in Poland,
"ceea ce avem nevoie în viata" in Romania,
"Ono što mi treba u Ïivotu" in Serbia,
"Wat ons in die lewe nodig het" in Afrikaans,
"Mga Kailangang ispiritwal sa buhay" in the Philippines—

For we all know women's rights are in the interest of all,
what we women need in life is what we all need in life,
because when women are finally treated fairly in the world,
when we're finally out from under your thumb,
when we finally aren't threatened by the violence of men,
when women are no longer degraded and are raised to equal footing,
when women are raised, we all*all* are raised
we are all better with fairness and equality,
where we can all grow, together

Image Index

The "Keeps Repeating" Instagram image was photographed in Clark Hall, Urbana, IL in 1991.

The "A Book for Men" images were photographed: of Claire in the late 1980s, of the cat Sequoia in 1995, of birds on an Austin, TX building edge in 2016, of the dog Wai Nai in 2003, of assorted grocery store produce in 2022, of a pumpkin outdoors 2008, of an outdoor garden tool and crack in street in 1990, of a bush in 2022, of holes photographed in Pompeii ruins in 2003, of the cat John Galt (Johnny) in boxes in 2005 (in the second photo with the cat Zach jumping through the image), of parts of doors from Stockholm, Sweden and Tallinn, Estonia in 2006, of bottles in 2022, of plastic bags in Helsinki, Finland in 2006, of Janet and Doug in 1990, of images of Janet and Chad in 1991, and of nails from 2004.

The front cover image is of Kuypers 4 December 2021 at the glass walkway in the Austin Public Central Library on César Chávez St. holding a steel mallet and wearing screws for earrings and a spanner for a ring (plus a "Rearden Steel" bracelet and a woman symbol pendant on a black chain), with pieces of glass separating the walkway from the camera.

The back cover image is a continuation for the glass walkway on the front cover, including smaller pictures (from top to bottom) of Janet Kuypers: with the name "Janet" written with henna in Hindi and Telugu on her arm, with the word "Scars" written on her arm with henna in Hindi, at the Taj Mahal in 2015, with a number of Chinese people who wanted their picture taken with her at the Great Wall of China (closest to Beijing) in 2004, swimming toward a sleeping shark at the Galapagos Islands in 2007, and doing a literal "polar plunge" into the Southern Ocean after camping in Antarctica in 2017.